A Room Full of Ghosts

As Hanna went behind the desk, other men she hadn't noticed before came up to her. "I'm a volunteer from Springfield, Illinois—Corporal Timothy McBain If you could get a message to my folks . . ."

"Me too," cried another Union man, coming toward her. There was something odd about how he moved. But then again, the light was dim. Obviously she hadn't seen right. Hanna blinked hard and busied herself taking down addresses. Meanwhile more and more men were crowding in on her. One of them put his hand over hers—and she realized she could see right through it.

"They're dead," Hanna told herself.

ESCAPE FROM GHOST HOTEL

Larry Weinberg

To Dori and Paula

ONE

There had been fifteen candles on Anna's birthday cake. "The five green ones," Mrs. Post explained as she set the cake in front of her, "are for the wonderful years since we found you in that field and took you home and you became our child. The nine pinks are for the years that you were with your first parents, may God rest their souls. The unlit candle in the middle was Kevin's idea. That one is for all the years in between that you skipped over when you came to us from out of the past."

"I told Mom not to light it because that's when you were neither dead nor alive. A whole hundred and fifty years in the Twilight Zone!" Anna's younger brother, Kevin, exclaimed.

Anna didn't like the weird expression on his face. "Don't make such a big thing of it, Kevin. I was never in any Twilight Zone. One minute I was back there being shot at, running for my life. The next I was here in the future, safe. It happened in a flash."

"Well, I don't think so or else you wouldn't have forgotten everything. Look how long it took before you even figured out that you were Hanna Terwilliger. And even then it was a couple of ghosts who had to tell you."

Anna glared at him. "Those weren't just ghosts. They were my mama and papa!"

"Well, it might have been nice if you'd let me meet them too! I was there in that creepy hotel just like you."

"There wasn't anything creepy about it, Kevin. The night we found it, everybody thought it was a nice little hotel in Indiana that had been turned into a museum because runaway slaves had been hidden in it before the Civil War. And I resent you calling it creepy when I was born right there and that used to be *my* home!"

"Yes, Kevin, *really!*" exclaimed Mrs. Post. "Why must you two always fight?"

"Mom, I'm not fighting! I only meant the place was haunted."

"Just by my parents, Kevin, not anybody else. And the only reason that their ghosts wouldn't lie still in their graves was because they thought I'd been murdered by those men who shot at me, but after they grew old and died they couldn't find me among the dead. They kept going back to the hotel, hoping I'd show up alive one day. After I did, they could finally rest in peace. So the Terwilliger Hotel isn't any more haunted now than *this* house is!"

"Oh, I don't know about that," sighed Mr. Post. "Sometimes I get the feeling that this house is haunted by the ghosts of Children's Quarrels Past. Now, in the interest of this cake not going into nuclear chocolate meltdown, Birthday Girl, won't you kindly blow out the candles?"

"Sure, Dad. Sorry," said Anna, quickly returning to good humor. As she blew them out, the family sang "Happy Birthday" and Mrs. Post began to cut the slices.

Kevin, though, was still scowling. He stuffed some cake

into his mouth and growled, "Maybe that place wasn't so strange when you were living there as Hanna Terwilliger. But you show me a tunnel going from a graveyard to *our* basement in this house that takes you back in time! You tell me there's nothing strange about *that?*"

"Talking while a big chunk of cake is rolling around in your mouth like clothes in a dryer—now *that*, Kevin, is strange."

Kevin gulped down his cake. "You didn't answer my question."

"Yes, it's strange." Anna waggled a fork at him. "But no stranger than my jumping ahead in time while I was running away from those men with guns. But *strange* doesn't mean creepy or haunted."

"What does it mean?"

"I don't know. Magic maybe." Growing thoughtful, she added, "Someone was helping me with magic."

Mr. Post leaned across the table. "Who do you think it was?"

They all waited, but a feeling was starting to come over Anna that this was a secret not to be revealed. "I . . . uh . . . I can't talk about it."

Anna's long silence and her faraway stare were beginning to get on everyone's nerves, particularly Mrs. Post's. "Are you thinking what I'm thinking, Anna? Because, if you are—"

"Barbara, what are you talking about?" asked her husband.

"Can't you guess? Just look at her. She wants to go back down to Indiana, climb into that empty grave, and crawl back through that collapsing tunnel again!"

Allan Post took a deep, troubled breath. "Is this true, Anna?"

Anna's lips trembled. She was close to tears. "I never got to say good-bye to them while they were alive! I never got to hold them . . . or . . . or . . . anything."

Mr. and Mrs. Post exchanged glances. Then he said, "Anna, you know that I've kept in touch with the sheriff in Indiana. Several kids have tried crawling into that tunnel, and one of them had to be taken to the hospital. I didn't want to tell you this before, but the police have caved in the tunnel and permanently sealed off the mouth. You couldn't get through there now no matter how hard you tried."

Anna stared in disbelief at her father for a long moment, then shouted, "That's unfair! That's my home! That's *my* tunnel!"

Bolting from the chair, she ran out of the kitchen and up to her room. She threw herself facedown on the bed. "I can never go back to them now. Never! Never! I'll never see Mama and Papa again!"

The face of a certain smoky-eyed little boy suddenly entered her mind. "No, or Rafe either," she cried, just before the sobs burst forth.

Rafe Sims was a runaway slave child the Terwilligers had been hiding in the hotel until men with guns came from Kentucky plantation country across the river. But it wasn't Rafe the trackers were looking for. It was his mother. Rosalie Sims was a freed black woman who had been searching for Rafe for years. When the Southern slave owners found out that she was actually Mother Freedom, a leader of the

Underground Railroad, they put a price on her head.

Rafe had slipped out of that escape tunnel and through the graveyard to meet his mama in the woods so they could flee to Canada. But when Hanna went after him, she saw the slave trackers following the boy out of the graveyard. She saw them shoot down his mother, and she grabbed little Rafe by the hand and ran with him. As the bullets flew at them the terrified Hanna let go of his hand and crossed over into the future as Anna . . . alone.

But the ghosts of Dora and Amos Terwilliger had drawn her back to the tunnel . . . and back into the past, giving Hanna the chance to relive the shooting of Mother Freedom. And this time Hanna did *not* let go. Hanna brought Rafe with her into the 1990s, to live with the Posts and to go to school at a time when there were no slaves.

But Rafe could never stop wondering if it was possible to save his mother, just as the girl whom he alone called "Hanna-Anna" had saved him. And so one day, when the family was revisiting the old hotel, Rafe went back into time, found his mother still alive, and stayed with her to work and fight against all the horrors of slavery. No, it wasn't just her parents whom Anna missed.

But Anna was also aware that she had blessings right here. The Posts, whom she also loved with all her heart, were still downstairs, and she had wrecked the little party they'd given for her. Pulling herself together she went down to them, kissed them all—even Kevin, the pest—and helped make the rest of the evening fun for the family.

Still, that terrible feeling of being cut off from her past

wouldn't go away. When she went back to bed that night, Anna had trouble falling asleep. And when she finally did, her dreams were so restless that some time during the middle of the night, she kicked off all her covers.

The window was open and the temperature outside was going down, down, down. Shivering, but still half asleep, Anna groped for the blankets and drew them around her. That was enough to let her sink back into her dreams. A freezing blast of wind sent the window shade rattling and crackling like a thing gone mad . . . and still she clung to sleep.

It was the loud snap of the shade suddenly rolling up by itself that made Anna's eyes open at last. But what caused her to sit straight up in the bed and spring to the door was the frost covering the window pane. In the early light of dawn, that frost was rapidly rearranging itself into a woman's face.

"Child, you hold on there," said the icy face. "Ain't I gone to enough trouble already without I has to chase you all over this house?"

"Who are you?"

"Oh, you goin' to 'member me presently. An' don't you be lookin' at me like I is a ghost already, 'cause I ain't. But now you'd best do like I tells you afore the sun come up and melts this here head of mine clean away. Go over to where you keeps what you needs to draw one of dem pictures you does so good. You 'n' me is goin' to make some magic together so you kin skip over just like you wants to. You knows who talkin' to you *now*, don't you?"

"Conjure Woman?"

"That's right."

She waited while Anna quickly grabbed a sketch pad and charcoal pencil from her desk. "Fine. Here's what you do. Sit y'self down in that chair an' draw my old-timey cabin wit' my old-timey porch onto the front of it and that good ol' cane rockin' chair onto the porch which I do so likes to sit in."

"I really don't remember it."

"Sho' you does. You was there that time you come wit' your mama to buy some of my potion for Mother Freedom when she come down wit' the heart sickness."

Drawing as fast as she could, Anna made the outlines of a cabin, porch, and chair. She held it up. "Like this?"

"That good enough, child. You don't have to fill no more in. What else does you 'member? Does you 'member anything of your own?"

"Well, there was a big pot on a fire on the ground outside. Something was boiling."

"All right. Draw that in. What was in that pot?"

"I don't know, but it tickled my nose."

"That was my head cold remedy: sassafras and some roots, child. I wants you to take one big sniff of that tickly stuff right now."

Anna's nostrils curled and she sneezed.

"Oh, you gettin' into it real good."

"There were some chickens wandering around too. They were everywhere."

"Oh, yeah, always chickens. Put just one o' dem onto it.

13

You don't have to bother wit' the feathers. Dem is pretty scraggly chickens anyhow. My, you sure can draw up a storm. Why you stoppin'—you think you finished?"

"Trees?"

"Yes, but ain't no time for trees now. It gettin' lighter out here an' I'm startin' to feel some sun already. Now what else ain't been put into that picture yet? What else be missin'?"

"I don't know."

"*You* is what's missin'. Hurry up now and put y'self into that picture. What you leaning over that mirror for?"

"I have to study my face."

"No, all you has to do is believe that's you. Now is that you?"

"I guess."

"Say it like you lives there, child."

"I reckon."

"Well, don't just reckon. Get y'self inside that picture of you."

"But how?"

"Oh, my, you makin' this hard for me. Don't you know yet you got the *Powers?* I can do some pullin' but you got to do some *pushin'*. Get your whole self into that picture, 'cause I ain't got no more time to stay wit' you. Take a step onto that porch."

"I'm trying. But I can't!"

"Sho' you kin. Them Powers was born right into you. I seen that much the first time ever I lay eyes on you. Li'l Rafe, now, I was able to teach him a trick or two, but he don't have the Powers like what you got. You just 'fraid to let y'self go, that's all. Well, I done all I can. You can see how I'm a-meltin'."

Anna turned desperately to the window, but already the face was dissolving into water.

"But I just don't know what to do!"

Faintly and from far off, she heard. "Spin . . ."

Anna ran to the window, calling into the wind. "What did you say? Did you tell me to spin?"

There was no answer. But spinning was all she could think of. And so Anna spread out her arms and began to twirl.

Nothing happened. Not a thing! She twirled harder, faster. She bumped into her dresser, into her bed. She was getting bruised. Still nothing! And from her parents' room came the cry of "What in the world is going on in there?"

Someone was walking toward her door. Anna became a twirling top. The whole room spun crazily in the other direction. It was all a blur. Anna glimpsed her mother at the door, calling, "Anna, stop it!" But she couldn't stop it. She wouldn't stop it. Not until her bare foot hit something soft, something that flew up in her face, squawking!

With those wings beating against her, she lurched to the side—straight into a rocking chair that went clattering to a plank floor with her on top of it.

"That you child? You done made it already?"

"Yes, I . . . I reckon so." She got to her feet.

"Well, good. My little trick worked."

"Trick?" repeated Hanna, looking around for the Conjure Woman.

"It sho' warn't the spinnin' what made you skip back.

15

Uh-uh. You done it with the Powers. Now come on over here so I kin see you one las' time 'fore I die."

"Where are you?"

"Don't look for me on top o' the groun', child. They is a hole by the willow tree. See it?"

Hanna hurried over to a pit. Gazing down, she saw the tiny, frail body of the Conjure Woman lying flat on her back with her arms crossed. "What are you doing down there?"

"This is my grave, child."

"But you said you weren't a ghost."

"No, I ain't—not yet. Running Deer, she dug this for me. She come when I'm gone an' do some cryin' an' say a Christian prayer when she cover me and send me off real nice with an Indian song-dance too. That dear soul woulda liked to stay wit' me till the end. But I told her to go along back to her nursing at the army hospital. You know where that is?"

"No, ma'am."

"It's the Terwilliger Hotel. Your mama turn it into a hospital soon after your papa went off to the war."

"The war? I've come back to the time of the *Civil War?*"

"Child, I don't know what to call it. But it's been a long fight, with so many boys on both sides a-cuttin' each other down till it breaks my heart. Us old ones gets to sit aroun' whilst all the big, strong, young ones is dyin' ahead of us. Why, that is the big shame of it. They say this here war just might put an end to slavery. An' that's why Rafe come down from Canada—to be a part of it. But he ain't found no sign-up place hereabouts that will take on a black man for a

16

soldier, an' meanwhiles they found out he a runaway slave. So the sheriff arrested him. They goin' ship him back to his master down in Kentuck."

"What? You mean they're still doing that *now*? I can't believe this!"

"Well, I told myself that too. But it happenin' all the same—an' lots of other bad things too. The North is all mixed up, child. Lots of white folks up here in Indiana ain't never been against slavery. And some of them is madder than hornets against black folks 'cause they blames us for the war. They hates Mr. Lincoln so bad that they goin' do anything they kin behind his back to make the Union lose. They's called Copperheads, child, like the poison snakes, and they's plenty of them in this county, tha's for sure. The sheriff mus' be one of them hisself, the way he beatin' on poor Rafe behind them bars. I knows it be going on 'cause I feels it. I kin always feel that boy, he so deep in me now." She gazed up at Hanna. "You feels him sometimes, don't you, sweetness?"

"Yes, ma'am, I surely do. But you have Powers. Can't you stop it?"

That old head shook slowly. "No, child. Oh, I has a few tricks now and then. But the Powers is just for doin' a little extra seein' into the darkness. Seein' an' movin'. Also a little bit of special healing now an' then, things like that. But maybe you kin help him."

"How?"

"Go along an' get your mama to put some money into that sheriff's pocket so she kin smuggle Rafe away from here again. Or else have her lawyer do up some kinda writ."

"Doesn't Mama know about this already?"

"Them Copperheads does lots of things in secret, child. Like night ridin' against the black folks and setting fires to the churches, things like that. Ain't nobody knows 'bout this one but me—and now you, Hanna."

"What about that nice pastor who hid Rosalie and Rafe and Mama and me in his ice wagon that time? He seemed to know everything that was going on."

"He was shot dead by some white men weeks ago when he tried to read them something 'bout the rights of man. You got to do somethin' right quick 'bout Rafe, 'cause they beatin' him in that jail somethin' terrible. I kin feels it each time, an' it's hurting me so I cain't stand it no more."

"Is that why you're dying?"

"Well, some of it, maybe. But child, I was way over a hundred years ol' the las' time you saw me on this side of time. And that was long ago. I don't want to cut wood no more an' cook no more an' clean no more an' sell potions and teas no more."

"You don't have to! Soon as I'm through with this, I'll take care of you!"

"Doesn't you wants to skip ahead again?"

"Yes, but we can do that together. You can have Rafe's old room, and a television set of your own. And somebody will always be around to drive you anywhere. My father is into history, and so is my friend Rafael. Would you believe he's the great-great grandson of Rafe! They'd just fall all over you."

"Uh-huh. Well, God bless you, child, but I'm stayin' put right here. And iffen you all wants to see me after I is dead, why I kin always come and haunt you." Suddenly she groaned. "You'd best get goin' now."

"But I can't just leave you like this."

"You has to. You is Hanna Terwilliger again, child. That name, it goin' to help you now. But you best hurry."

TWO

Hanna did try to hurry along the twisting path that led away from that clearing in the backwoods of Indiana. But she was no longer the small child who could race barefoot over roots and rocks without noticing them. They soon slowed her down to a walk. By the time she came upon a horse and buggy road, she was hobbling painfully.

The road was full of jagged pebbles too, but there were grassy patches along the edges, and some dried horse droppings in the middle to softly step on. Hanna's next problem was whether to head left or right to get to town. Mama had driven her out this way to buy Rosalie's medicine, but Hanna hadn't been paying any attention to directions then. She only remembered that it was a pretty long ride past open farm country on either side. Well, there were no farms here, only more woods in any direction she looked. Hanna closed her eyes.

Now wasn't this silly? Why take the notion that just because there was an itch starting up on the right side of her nose she should go to the right? Still, she might as well try it.

The road took a bend, and through the thinning trees she began to see more sunlight. Rounding the second bend, Hanna saw a field of corn. Deep in the middle of it, under a wide straw hat, a raggedy scarecrow stretched its arms over a long broomstick.

Hanna stopped and stared at the torn, faded blue overalls and red-checkered shirt the scarecrow was wearing. Then she headed into the field, thinking it was better to go into town in those than wearing her pajamas!

Surely it was just her imagination, but the scarecrow's button eyes seemed to grow wary as she came closer and started to undo the shoulder straps. "Now don' be upset with me," she said as she rolled down the coveralls. "You're getting the better of this deal."

"Who says I want it?" piped a muffled voice. Hanna nearly jumped out of her skin.

"Now you put everythang back on me, and you git."

Hanna realized that the voice was coming from somewhere nearby in the high corn. It was a child's voice.

"Hello, there. You sure scared me."

"I'll bet I did!"

"I think I know where you are now."

"No, you don't," the voice declared firmly.

"Look, do you see what I'm wearing? They're almost new, not torn or anything. Won't you let me trade with him for these?"

"What fer?" said the voice.

"Well, I have to get to town, you see. But I can't do it in these."

"Why not?"

"Because these are bedclothes."

"Bedclothes?" repeated the moving voice. "They sure don't look it."

22

"Well, they are. They're called pajamas."

"So what are you doing goin' around in your bedclothes?"

"That's just my problem."

"Well, it shore ain't my scarecrow's problem."

"That's true," declared Hanna in a defeated voice, and she started to turn away.

"Just one blame minute! Kin I touch 'em first?"

"Sure, if you'll stand up and let me see you."

"Nothing doin'," said the voice.

"Then I'm going."

Quick as a hummingbird, a hand darted out about knee high, then pulled back again. "Ohhh," said the voice when the hand retreated. "Those thangs are soooo soft!"

Hanna stopped walking. "They should be. They're made of silk."

"Silk!" exclaimed the child. "You mean from Paris, France?"

"No, I think it's from China."

"Well, I ain't got to that in geography yet. Is it far?"

"Oh, very far." Hanna fell silent for a moment. "You know, I wonder if my old teacher, Mr. Weems, is still—"

"My sakes, you went to him too?" At this, a girl about ten years old, dressed not much differently from the scarecrow, jumped up. "You went to him too?"

"I surely did. Every time he caught me drawing pictures in my composition book instead of writing, I'd get a whack over my knuckles with his ruler."

"Oh, that hain't nothing to what he does to the boys with his cane. He is somethin' fierce sometimes."

23

Hanna nodded. "Does he still make all the classes read aloud from their different primers at the same time?"

"Well, of course he does. What a foolish question. How long have you been gone from there?"

"Depending how you look at it, either a few years or a lot. Now listen, I've got to be going. Do we make the trade or not?"

"Won't tell you that till I find out why you want to trade silk from China for ratty-tatty scarecrow thangs."

"Good question, but it's hard to explain."

"Try it." The child crossed her arms.

"Well, I've been spending time way in the future, about a hundred fifty years from now. But I came back for a short visit, only I didn't get the chance to get into the right clothes."

"Heck," said the girl. "Iffen I was a-goin' to spin a tall one, I could do a lot better 'n that. But that's all right—it's still a trade. You wait right here. I'm gonna brang you some of my sister's thangs that oughta fit you jest fine." Turning in the direction of a split-log farmhouse at the far end of the field, she broke into a run.

Hanna called after her. "Won't your sister mind?"

"She would iffen she could come back for 'em," the girl called over her shoulder. "But my pap won't allow it, 'cause she's a fallen woman!"

Hanna turned from watching her to study the road. It was still empty in both directions, and she had no idea how long it would take to get to town. Her thoughts wandered until the distant crack of a closing door made her look around.

The girl was hurrying back with a fluffy bundle in front of her.

"These was her best Sunday-go-to-meeting thangs," the girl called as she ran up. "Pap spent all his savings on buying 'em when he was a-hopin' she'd catch Preacher Osgood after he buried his third wife. Only the preacher's got children that are older'n her, so she run off to marry a soldier."

"That's why she's a fallen woman?"

"Yes! And also 'cause her feller is in the Union Army and my pap was born in the South. So here's a blouse an' a skirt and a petticoat and a matchin' bonnet and shoes and a beaded string purse, only they's no money in it."

"Well, I should think not. But those are much too nice. Don't you want to keep them until you get big enough to wear them yourself?"

"Well, I hate shoes and I 'spect I'll always hate 'em. The rest might be all right, I guess, but I'll never git to wear them anyhow. Pap keeps sayin' as how he's a-goin' to burn them. An' he will too. Every time he gets drunk I have to hide them in a different place, but I'm running out of places. So here, let's swap. If you is shy about undressin' I promise I won't look—though I've seen all kinds of animals naked."

Hanna laughed as she crouched behind the scarecrow. "Well, I should think you would have. But still, I wouldn't want to be seen from the road."

"Why, you kin wait all day and not be seen from that ol' road. So my name is Binny Drover. What's yours?"

"I have two of them. Anna Post and Hanna Terwilliger."

"Well, Terwilliger I think I know. There was a girl who

25

went to our school before I got there. Schoolteacher Weems says she had something to do with a thang called the Underground something. And he said she was shot at by slave trackers right in front of his cabin whilst he was away. But nobody ever found the body."

"They didn't find it because she wasn't killed," Hanna declared.

"How do you know?"

"Because," said Hanna, reaching for the bonnet, "that was me."

Binny's eyes bulged. "That was *you?*"

"It surely was."

"Oh, come on now!"

"I'm telling the truth." Hanna spread her arms and turned around for inspection. "So what do you think?"

"You ain't her!"

"I am."

"Where have you been all this time?"

"Well, I lost my memory for a while."

"How old are you now?" the girl demanded.

"Fourteen."

"Then you cain't be her! She were about eight or nine when she disappeared, and that was way back in—"

"Eighteen fifty. Sometimes when I skip through time, I end up a different age than I should be. What year is it now?"

"You don't know?"

"Not exactly."

"You don't know this is 1862?"

26

"What month?"

"What *month?* Look at the corn. How high is it?"

"August?"

"Oh, I see what you're a-tryin' to do. You're a changin' the subjec'. But it won't work. I see right through this tall story too. So give it up, 'cause you just ain't good at it."

Hanna lifted an eyebrow. "Had you fooled for a while though, didn't I?"

"Did not."

"Did too. 'Fess up."

"Won't neither. Anyways, I got to go and build a fire afore Pap wakes up sober. Then I'll cry a little bit so he'll think this time he really did go and burn them clothes."

"That's kind of sad," said Hanna.

"Well, it is. But then maybe my pap will start to feel sorry about it. And if he's real sorry, then I kin show him the letters from my sister the postman's been a-hidin' under a tree stump for me so Pap won't tear them up."

Binny had brightened considerably, and Hanna held out her hand, asking, "How are you going to explain your new pajamas?"

"Won't have to. I'll keep 'em under my covers and only put 'em on when I'm in bed! Now listen, you come back again, and I'll teach you how to really tell some tall ones!"

"I'll try!"

Hanna went down to the road in Binny's sister's rather large shoes. Just before the next bend she looked back. Binny was still standing by the scarecrow. They gave each other a parting wave, and the girl hurried toward the house.

Hanna walked on and on, with nary a rider on horseback or a passing carriage or anyone walking in either direction. Meanwhile, the morning sun climbed higher in the sky. There was not the slightest breeze, and the growing heat made the air turn hazy.

Little by little, her mind began to swim. The sunlight dazzled her eyes, leaving dancing spots in front of them. Her steps grew confused, and she wove this way and that on the road. She barely noticed the clopping of hoofs until a black man driving a wagonload of hay came alongside and halted his mule, saying, "Always room for one more, if you care to."

She looked at him groggily. "Excuse me, sir? What did you say?"

"My, you are polite. I like that." He leaned across the seat. "Here, let me give you a hand up. If you put that bonnet in your lap and open this old parasol I keep under the seat, you'll cool your head and get some better shade."

"Thank you," Hanna murmured as she began to study his face. When she saw him noticing, she said, "For a moment you reminded me of someone. He was a pastor, but he used to drive a wagon too. It was an ice wagon."

He looked at her more closely. "You knew Reverend McWilliam?"

"Yes, I did."

"Well, he is very sadly missed. He taught many of us to read and write, and so much more besides. And he was brave in every way."

"Such a good man," she cried, "and they burned his church and murdered him!"

The driver turned halfway around in his seat. "I am very surprised. White folks here don't pay any attention to what happens to any of us. It's like they don't even know what's going on. And when I try to tell them, they look away and say, 'Oh, Moses, you can't be right. That sort of thing doesn't go on up here in the North. It must have been an accident or something some crazy person is doing.'

"'Then there are many crazy persons,' I say. 'They come in the night with masks on and torches in their hands, and they call themselves the Knights of the Golden Circle. Surely you must have heard them ride past your door last night.' But they shake their heads, and that's when they tell me they won't be needing any more hay from me, thank you very much, and I shouldn't go around upsetting folks with these wild stories. So, young lady, I thank you for believing it, and I wonder who told you."

"A lady I know."

"I begin to think I know who that lady is and where you've been walking from. Who are you?"

"I'm not sure you would understand."

"If you got anything to do with the Conjure Woman, I might."

"My name is Hanna Terwilliger."

"If you are a relation to the Colonel and Mrs. Terwilliger, then you come from a family I respect very much."

"Thank you, I am. Do you know the name Rafe Sims?"

"Hmm. Seems like I should."

"Mother Freedom's son."

"My Lord, yes, that little slave boy. The one the reverend

hid before he was taken to Canada. I am one of the church deacons, you know. We're all meeting in my haybarn until we can build again. Tell me about Rafe Sims. He must be a young man of about twenty by now. Is he still up in Canada?"

Hanna shook her head. "He came down to join the army, but he got arrested first. He's in the jail, and they're beating him and they want to send him back to his old master in Kentucky!"

"Why that's horrible. *Horrible!* And I didn't even know."

"I can't understand it. How can they still be sending runaways back with the war on?"

"Oh, they wouldn't dare do it if he came from any of the rebel states. But Kentucky has stayed with the Union. So have Tennessee and Maryland, and they're all keeping their slaves. It's still the law."

"Well, I can't let Rafe go back!" Hanna cried. "I just can't!"

The deacon had grown very upset. "Those Knights of the Golden Circle I mentioned—the reason we can't get them brought to justice is that their leader is the deputy who is in charge of that jail. The sheriff himself is afraid of the man! And if Mother Freedom's son is in the hands of someone like that, I don't give two cents for his life!"

30

THREE

The deacon didn't think it would do for them to be seen entering town together, so Hanna got off the haywagon a little distance before and walked to the jail. It was a solid brick building with a single, tiny window too high for her to glance inside. She and the deacon had discussed how she should approach her task. She knocked on the door.

"How-de-do," she said, offering a pretty little curtsey to the big brute of a man who opened it. "I am the daughter of Squire Bowes of the Bowes Plantation down in Kentucky. May I come inside?"

"No."

"Well, then we can talk out here."

"Sheriff does the talking. The office is back of the courthouse."

He was about to close the door in her face when she called out quickly, "I understand that, suh. But I believe you are holding a runaway belonging to my daddy."

"Is that right?"

"Well, my daddy says it is. He asked me to stop by on my way to visit my married sister up in Indianapolis. Daddy says he got a letter that you've finally caught that—now what in the world was the boy's name? I was so small when he ran away that I hardly recall. Oh, yes, Rafe Sims. Daddy is very grateful for his capture, and he wanted me to say so in person to everybody who was involved in it. Mostly, though, he wants to be sure that when we get that boy returned to us, he will be in good enough condition to pull a plow and be worth the reward money we are paying you for him."

"I ain't being paid nothing for him," barked the man. "Sheriff don't share his reward with me. Likewise, I don't let him tell me how to run my jail."

"You mean to say you don't get *any* of it? Why, I am scandalized. That's not fair to you at all! The sheriff only had to arrest this criminal, but you're the one who has to keep him from getting away. You certainly should get some money for yourself, and I am going to see to it that you do."

The keeper rubbed his unshaven chin. "How much are we talkin' about here?"

"Two hundred dollars. Would that suit you?"

"Reckon it could be done private?"

"Oh, yes."

"When do I see the money?"

The deacon had suggested she stretch the time out as long as possible. "Um . . . day after tomorrow."

"I thought you was just passin' through."

"Well, yes, but I am staying in town a few days."

"Where?"

Hanna's mind was a blank. What was the name of that white minister Binny's pa had wanted her sister to marry? "With . . . the Preacher Osgood," she said.

He stared at her. "That a fact?"

"Yes, suh, it is. His last wife—you know, the third one—

well, she was kin to us Bowes, poor dear, but we never got to the funeral. I—"

"That's enough talking. If you don't have that money for me now, how are you goin' to git it?"

"Oh, I will! Yes, I will. It's just a matter of . . . going down to the bank."

"Then I don't see why you can't do that tomorrow."

"All right then, tomorrow."

"Make it two hundred and fifty."

She was about to agree, but something told her to haggle. "Oh, well, I don't know about *that* much."

"Now you listen here," the deputy said very slowly and straight into her face. "So far, I been going easy on this here boy. But I don't know how long I can keep on holding my temper. He thinks he got a right to put on a white man's uniform and go marchin' off to shoot at other white men! But I've got just the right thing here to put a stop to all his thinking permanent."

He slapped at the little leather sack that was hanging over his belt, and she could hear the rocks inside cracking together.

"I understand your feelings," Hanna said, though it was all she could do to keep her voice steady. "But he is my daddy's property and not anybody else's to do with as they please. Still, you can be sure that if he ever dares to give us any kind of trouble again my daddy will bullwhip him and then hang him from the highest tree to set an example for the other coloreds. You can have that two hundred and fifty dollars. But I do need to see him now."

33

"Well, all right," grumbled the deputy. "But I don't know how conscious he is. He got a little uppity with me last night, and I had to show him why that wasn't such a good idea. He ain't been moving since. Might be pretending 'bout that, though. Come with me."

The man led her through his office. Then he unlocked an iron gate and they entered a small space. On the other side of it were the bars of two cells. Only one had a window. It was clean, with sunlight pouring into it and a cot with a blanket for a prisoner to lie on. That cell was empty. The other cell was in shadows. It had no cot, no blanket, and it stank like an unwashed toilet. On the floor, curled up on his side, lay a young man with chains on his legs and manacles on his wrists.

"On your feet!" bawled the keeper. "Rise and shine!"

He didn't move, did not even seem to be breathing. Hanna had to force down a scream.

"Rafe . . . little Rafe Sims," she called to that form lying still as death on the floor. "You stop playing those sly Brer Rabbit ways of yours. We are both too big for that now. I was awful good to you. And you've got to beg my forgiveness for doing such a mean and spiteful thing as running away from my daddy and the plantation. Now don't you just lie there pretending you don't know the sound of my voice. Y'all know it perfectly well."

He didn't stir. Hanna turned to the jailer. "Just how hard *did* you hit him last night?"

"Oh, a tap or two is all. Maybe he just don't want to go back to that plantation of yours. He must want to stay here with me. Ain't that right, boy? You like it here in my jail?"

She went to the bars. "Now you listen, Rafe Sims! You cheated our plantation out of too many good days of work already, and you are going back where you belong. Do you hear what Hanna-Anna is telling you?" She turned to the jailer, explaining. "That's what they called me when I was small."

"Is it now? Well maybe then his brains—if he ever had any—is just a mite scrambled. Oh, there he goes, he's a-movin' now."

Rafe's head lifted ever so slightly from the floor. Then it dropped back, and there was nothing.

Hanna bit down on her lip hard enough to taste blood. She was desperate. Was there no way to reach him? She had never known a day when Rafe wasn't on fire inside. That fire had to be there no matter how often and how badly he'd been beaten! Suddenly she cried out, "Rafe Sims, how many children do you have?"

When the guard looked at her, she explained. "They belong to our plantation just like he does. I want to know about my property."

"That's right." He slammed the bars with his club, shouting, "Don't make me come in there now, boy. You got children?"

The prisoner barely shook his head.

"Well, I think you're lying," Hanna declared. "Because I heard that you do. And I also heard that you tell them tall stories about when you lived in the future, and how black people could go to school and vote and be citizens."

"That'll be the day," sneered the deputy.

But Hanna went on. "Yes, and you told them how there was a man named Martin Luther King who said he'd been to the mountaintop and that he had a dream!"

Rafe was lifting his head and trying to move his swollen, blood-caked lips. A low sound came from them, impossible to make out. He licked his lips and tried again. "No children, Hanna-Anna."

"Missy Hanna-Anna to you!" bellowed the keeper.

"Well, you *will* have children," she cried, trying to meet his eyes in the shadows. "I surely predict you will. And grandchildren too, and grandchildren of your grandchildren. And one of them will look and sound just like—"

Hanna could feel the deputy studying her. "And all of them are going to work at our plantation so they can pay my family back for all the trouble you put us to," she said quickly. "So you'd better get your strength together, you hear me?"

"I hear you, *Missy Hanna-Anna*," Rafe whispered. "Awful good to see you too."

Hanna swallowed hard. "I'll be back," she said, though she dared not say it softly.

But he was struggling to sit up. And even in the semidarkness there was one thing she could make out. That stubborn, smoky look she knew so well was coming back into his eyes.

"Before you go off laughin', there's something I want you to know," said the deputy as he walked her to the outside door. "You just finished him off."

36

Hanna stopped in her tracks. "What do you mean?"

"You two may think I'm stupid, but I know you was talking in some kind of code. And I don't believe you're who you say you are."

"Look, I'll get you that two hundred fifty if you leave him alone! I'll make it a *thousand* if you let him go!"

"Who'll you get it from?"

"Never you mind."

"You trying to bribe an officer? That's a crime!"

"You're going to arrest me? I don't think so! My father is Colonel Amos Terwilliger of the United States Army."

"Everybody knows he had but one child and she's dead!"

"Well, they're wrong. And if you think there's nobody in this part of Indiana except Copperhead traitors like you, you're wrong too! So you'd better let him alone from now on, or—"

"Or what?" The padded bag of rocks was suddenly in his hand.

"You'd better not! Too many people came with me."

"That right? How come I didn't see any?"

"Who sees you and your murdering Knights of the Golden Circle?"

"You cain't prove nothin'!" he said, shoving her through the door. "There's only two ways this boy leaves my jail—in a pine box or in chains, bound for Kentucky! Now get on out of here!"

Hanna raced down the hill toward the river landing. It was there that the road to her home began, and all the sobbing girl could think of now was getting to her mama.

Mama would know what to do for Rafe! And Mama needed to know she was alive!

She ran along the shore, barely noticing a long, bloodstained barge tied up at the dock. She rushed on until a troop of Union cavalry forced her to the side to let a line of covered wagons go by. Each wagon was filled to the top of its canvas roof with medical supplies. As the one in the lead rolled past, the woman at the reins gave her a curious, troubled look. But Hanna, still blurry-eyed with tears, did not see her.

The deacon had said he would meet her, and about a mile farther on he pulled his wagon out of a clearing. Hanna told him how desperate the situation at the jail was. "And I'm afraid I only made things worse!" she sobbed.

He put a fatherly arm around her shoulder. "Now that I know what's going on, I'll spread the word. Our brethren are coming out tonight, you see if we don't. We'll have a prayer vigil front of that jail for all to see. We're going to honor our dead brothers and sisters and stand up for our living ones. We're going to make the white folks around here finally decide which side of slavery and human decency they are on. Because we ain't leaving, come what may, till that young man walks on out of there free!"

Though the mule had been clopping along very slowly, they overtook another line of ambulances. These, however, were crammed full of wounded men who'd been carried off the barge on stretchers. The line had stopped moving. As they came to a halt behind it, Hanna asked, "Where was the battle?"

"Oh, somewhere down in Tennessee, I expect. There's a navy steamboat called *Red Rover* that takes them up the Mississippi to the big army hospital at Mound City on the Ohio River. But when there's too many soldiers left over, they get put on barges for the tugboats to haul to smaller hospitals like the one Mrs. Terwilliger set up here for a volunteer outfit called the Sanitary Commission."

A cavalry officer rode up and said, "Sorry, you can't get through this way, but you still have room here to turn around."

The deacon touched his cap. "Can I ask you, sir, what happened up yonder?"

"Two wagons went over when the axles broke off. They were sawed almost clean through, and if you ask me, Copperheads did it. Everything we don't stand guard over, they sneak around and get at The woods around here are thick with 'em."

"How come nobody asks us who they are?" the deacon said. "You put some more of my people in uniforms, and we'll root them out quicker than you can say Jack Robinson."

"Don't I wish I could," said the soldier before he rode off.

Hanna had already jumped down to take the mule by its bridle and lead it around in a small half-circle. The deacon shook his head. "You run on ahead. We both have things to do."

She thanked him. But as she stepped away, he called out, "Wait. How much money have you got?"

The question startled her. "Why, none. Please forgive me, but as soon as I get any, I'll pay you."

"Not for me. For you." He fished several coins from a pocket. "Here's eight bits. If you can use any more, I'll have some tonight." He held out his hand.

"That is so nice of you, but I won't need it."

"Yes, that's probably so," he said gently. "But I want you to take it, just in case."

It was hard for Hanna not to lower her eyes while edging past the open backs of those ambulances. She forced herself to look. Most of the men packed inside lay on their backs as if they were already dead. The few who were sitting up were covered in bandages. But there was one soldier—just a boy really—who seemed perfectly all right. He sat blowing softly on a bugle, his legs dangling off the back of a wagon. Hanna smiled at him. It was only when he did not smile back that she realized the boy was blind.

From an ambulance just ahead, a woman shouted, "You there, you! Get in here quickly."

When Hanna stopped in confusion, the nurse stuck her head out, pointing an arm that was drenched to the elbow in blood. "Don't just stand there! I need help!"

Hanna did not want to help. She wanted nothing to do with all that gore! When she didn't move, the nurse called out for someone else. "Someone hurry or I'll lose this man! His stitches have burst and I've got a bayonet puncture spouting from the artery!"

Hanna sprang into the ambulance. A man lay on his stretcher, spurting blood from a gash above the left knee.

"Grab that leg and lift it. I know it's heavy but you'll

have to hold it high. I'm going to try to stop the blood flow with a tourniquet, then redo the stitches."

"But that's wrong, isn't it?"

"What is?"

"I really didn't study this. I just remember that tourniquets aren't a good idea."

"Just do as I tell you."

They worked together quickly. But when the nurse reached into her bag for silk thread to stitch with, Hanna objected again. "Excuse me, but I don't think you can just wipe the dirt off the needle on that piece of cloth. Doesn't it have to be sterilized?"

"Sterilized?" repeated the nurse. When Hanna saw her bewildered look, she realized that nobody at this time had ever heard of germs.

"Please, just trust me. Otherwise the wound will get infected. Do you have any alcohol?"

"No. Wounds always get infected. That's just part of the healing process."

"No, it isn't!"

The nurse whispered furiously in her ear. "You're making these men more fearful, and that's the worst thing you can do. Now control yourself! When I'm finished, I'll need you to give me a hand carrying him up the hill to the hospital. Are you strong enough to do that?"

"Yes."

The nurse worked swiftly, saying at last, "I don't know how long these will hold. Let's go. I'll take the front."

Stepping off first to take the heavier weight, the nurse

pulled at the stretcher. Hanna stooped to lift it from behind. It was backbreaking work, but she got it as far as the edge. Now came the problem of keeping hold of the stretcher while stepping down.

One of the other wounded men came cheerily to the rescue, saying, "Miss, you climb off and I'll hand him to you." He swiveled around on his stomach, explaining, "Those legs of mine stayed in Memphis, but these arms are good as ever. Sorry about your pretty clothes getting so messed up. But you give 'em a good quick scrubbing and they'll come out all right."

Hanna took her end of the stretcher and swung it around behind the nurse. As they went to the front of the ambulance with it, she saw why nobody else had rushed over to help. To the left began the carriage path that wound uphill to the hospital. Partway up, two broken ambulances had tipped over against the trees. Women nurses and male orderlies alike were frantically pulling wounded men out and carrying them toward the hospital as rapidly as possible.

"Can you keep holding him?" the nurse asked her as they slipped past the wagons to fall in behind the others.

Hanna didn't know how it was going to be possible. Her arms were trembling under their burden. "I can if you can," she grunted.

"Bigger doesn't always mean stronger. Were you coming here to volunteer?"

"To find my mother."

"Who is she?"

Hanna didn't hear the question. One more bend in the

path and she would see the high rooftop of home. There it was! New energy flowed into her as they took those last trudging steps to the level ground where the great, wide, grassy lawn of the hotel began.

Hanna stared in amazement. The lawn, with all its little footpaths, its benches for guests, and its balls and mallets for the game of croquet, was gone. In its place were long narrow buildings with low, flat roofs radiating from the old hotel's big porch and marble entrance like the spokes of a giant wheel. Soldiers on crutches were standing in front of one building, talking. A man with a bandaged head sat against an outside wall, puffing away at the corncob pipe that stuck out through the bandages around his mouth. Beside him sat another man busily writing a letter.

"Everything's changed," Hanna whispered to herself as they headed between two barracks to the place of her birth.

"Have you been here before?" the nurse asked.

"Yes."

"That's surprising. I thought I knew everyone in town. My name is Martha Vickers. My husband is Doctor Vickers." She hesitated and added, "Some people call me Running Deer."

Hanna recalled hearing that name. But where?

Two strong orderlies came rushing up to take their stretcher. "Let's get him to an operating room quickly," Running Deer told them and dashed on ahead.

Hanna followed in a sort of daze. There was something so unreal about all of this. The darkening of the late afternoon sky made it all even stranger. The patients who'd been lingering about looked up at the dark, thick clouds, then hobbled into their barracks to avoid the impending storm. Other recovering patients got up from wicker chairs on the porch. Hanna remembered those chairs from her earliest childhood. How well she recalled seated ladies with teacups in their hands, endlessly complaining about their clumsy servant girls back home. And men standing by the porch rail with brandy glasses and big cigars, chatting away with Papa about how the newfangled railroads were starting to put the riverboats out of business.

Big droplets were already starting to fall. Hanna worried about the deacon and how his hay would be ruined if he didn't have something to throw over it. But what a thing to think about now when she was going to see Mama at last! Why was she moving so slowly? What was she afraid of? A strange sense of dread was stealing over her, growing heavier than the sheets of rain that had begun to pour down behind her as she mounted the marble steps and went slowly inside.

The big lobby was the one thing that hadn't changed. There were the same large and beautiful white chairs. The old brass spittoons gleamed even in the darkening afternoon. The same tall plants that Mama used to let her water were sprouting from their lovely round boxes. The same tall desk of polished wood stood off to the right side, with the door behind it leading to Mama and Papa's room, and to her own. The knot in her stomach unwound and she began to breathe easier.

A voice from behind saying, "Pardon me, Miss," made her jump.

44

Hanna whirled around but saw only a young man in gray. "Oh, I am sorry, Miss. Didn't mean to scare you thataway. My name is Private Harley Briggs. They took me here though I'm a Johnny Reb. An' I am so worried 'bout my wife and baby back home. Do you think you could get a letter down to her in Birmingham, Alabama? It ain't like I kin write, y'see."

"No, I don't mind at all. Wait till I get some paper."

As Hanna went behind the desk, other men she hadn't noticed before came up to her. "I'm a volunteer from Springfield, Illinois—Corporal Timothy McBain. If you could get a message to my folks . . ."

"Yes, certainly."

"Me too," cried another Union man, coming toward her. There was something odd about how he moved. But then again, the light was dim. Obviously she hadn't seen right. Hanna blinked hard and busied herself taking down addresses. Meanwhile more and more men were crowding in on her. One of them put his hand over hers—and she realized she could see right through it.

"They're dead," Hanna told herself, trying hard not to let the pencil drop from her fingers. She had to force herself to keep writing, but the point broke from pressing on it too hard. "I'll get another pencil," she managed to say quietly. Most of the men seemed so calm and pleasant, she wondered whether they knew yet what had happened to them.

A scream of agony came from upstairs. It was loud and long, but it stopped suddenly. They all looked up. "Who is it? Who're they operating on?"

"That old sergeant major, I think. Hard a man as he is, I shore didn't expect him to put up that kind of a noise."

"Well, there's pain you kin stop with chloroform and pain that you cain't. But he's all right now, one way or the other, poor soul. We'll see iffen he comes floatin' down to join us."

A ghastly form appeared at the top of the stairs. "What happened? Did I make it? Am I dreaming or am I . . . ?" He couldn't bring himself to say the word.

"Sorry, Sergeant," one of the ghosts called up. "It's all over but the burying. Come on down here and get in line to send a message home. This here is a real kind soul who kin see ghosts, and she ain't afraid of us neither."

"Well, *I'm* afraid," cried a youthful voice from the darkest part of the lobby. "I've been dead for days and days, but I just can't bear the thought of it! I am so scared. So very—"

Another voice cut through his. It belonged to a woman in black who was rapidly entering from the passageway where the guest rooms used to be. "Get away from behind the desk," she snapped at Hanna. "That's my station and you have no right to be there!"

Her quick, angry steps scattered the ghosts like feathers in a high wind and made Hanna furious. "Did you have to charge right through them, sounding so nasty? You chased them away."

"Chased who away?"

"Corporal McBain! Private Harley Briggs! The sergeant who was just operated on! And all the others."

"What others?"

"The ones who've died!"

"Pull yourself together!" commanded the nurse, rushing around the desk to take her by the shoulders. "We do not allow ourselves to break down here. These men have suffered enough, and for their sakes we must be strong. You, I suppose, are the volunteer who brought in a patient with Nurse Vickers. That soldier is going to be all right, I think. Now I want you to get out of those bloody clothes this instant. Go through this door and down to the last room on the right. You'll find whatever you need there. When you come back, we'll sit you down in the commissary and give you something to settle your nerves."

"I . . . I have to find my mother."

"And who is she?"

"Dora Terwilliger."

The head nurse looked at her strangely. "Mrs. Terwilliger isn't here now."

"Tell me where I can find her. I have to do it right away."

"Dump those clothes into the laundering bin. Go now."

It was to Hanna's own room that she had been sent. She found it completely changed. Gone were the childhood toys that had been kept in the cradle Papa had carved out of hickory wood just before she was born. The cradle was gone too, and so was her bed, her dressing table, and the music box with the little blue horse on top that she'd named after the family's beloved carriage horse, Johnny Appleseed.

The room had been turned into a nurses' closet with two poles stretched across it. Long, black, pleated skirts hung on one side. White blouses with wide sleeves and high collars hung on the other. There were shelves for white petticoats and shelves for white aprons. The floor was covered with pairs of shoes that laced up to the ankles.

But the old rug was still there. As soon as Hanna had put on a clean uniform, she bent down to look under the rug for the trap door to the secret chamber. Pulling it up just a crack, she peered down into the blackness where runaways like Rafe used to be hidden. Was it possible he would have to be smuggled into that secret room once again? Could they even get him away from that jail? Where was Mama?

Someone was coming into the closet room. As she jumped up, the head nurse appeared, asking, "Why did you tell me that Dora Terwilliger is your mother?"

"She is."

"And who do you say you are?"

"*Hanna.*"

"That can't be right. Mrs. Terwilliger had only one child. She was murdered many years ago."

"Look, I can't explain it to you, but that's wrong," Hanna said. "I have to get her help to save someone very dear to me, and I must do it right away! Now please tell me where she is!"

"Mrs. Terwilliger has left with a dozen supply wagons for the battlefields in Tennessee. They went across the river on the barge that brought these last patients. I have no idea when she'll be back."

Hanna grew frantic. "Are you *sure* they've crossed already?"

"Now listen to me. We are having emergencies of all kinds breaking out here today. A moment ago you were talking to dead men, and now you're claiming to be a dead child!"

"I'm not dead!"

"Whatever you are, you're certainly very confused. I just cannot find the time right now to help you sort this out. I don't want you to go after her. I don't want you to trouble her. Those medical supplies are desperately needed by the troops at the front, and she is responsible for getting them there safely. Will you give me your word that you won't try to go after her?"

"You don't understand. I have to see her now!"

"Then I'm very sorry," the head nurse said, stepping backward out of the room. "But there's a padlock on this door, and I am going to keep you in here for a while."

Before Hanna could rush past her, the door had closed in her face and she heard the click of the lock. "I know this must be frightening for you," called the nurse in reassuring tones. "But just think of what those men on the operating tables upstairs are facing. Do try to bear up, and I will be back to let you out at the end of my shift. That window, I must tell you, would be dangerous to climb out of. It overhangs the cliff."

Almost before the woman stopped talking, Hanna had opened the secret trap door. She closed it above her and carefully lowered herself down the steep ladder into a darkness that was deeper than night. Crossing the stone floor with her hands out in front until they touched the far wall, she found the round mouth of the tunnel that Papa had dug for runaway slaves to enter and leave unseen.

Hanna gave a little shudder before getting down on her hands and knees. It wasn't because of the long, tight, almost airless crawl that lay ahead of her, or because the tunnel came out in the little graveyard down the hill from the hotel. It wasn't even that the last part of this tunnel *was* a grave, an empty one. It was what had been written on the tombstone the Terwilligers had placed there after she'd skipped ahead to become Anna Post that made her shiver:

THIS GRAVE LIES WAITING FOR OUR
DEARLY BELOVED CHILD, HANNA.
BORN 1841. DIED 1850.
BY SLAVEHUNTERS SOMEWHERE
CRUELLY MURDERED.

Hanna crawled into the tunnel, determined to keep her mind busy any way she could. And for a long time that wasn't too hard to do, not with all her worries about Rafe and being so anxious to catch up to Mama. But little by little a feeling began to grow that someone . . . or some*thing* . . . was right behind her. There was no possible way to put that out of her thoughts.

Finally, when she could stand the terror of it no more, Hanna screamed, "What do you want?"

"Take me with you," pleaded a young and ghostly voice.

"I can't!"

"But I don't want to be alone. I'm so afraid of being dead! I don't know what's going to happen to me."

"How old were you when you died?"

"I don't remember. I'm beginning to forget everything. That's part of what scares me."

"But maybe that's for the best."

"Do you really think so?"

"Of course—unless you want to go on like this." The tunnel was taking a slight turn upward. Hanna's raised hand touched the round hatch cover that had been disguised from above by a layer of earth. "I have to leave you," she said. "I'm very sorry that you didn't get to live out a long life. I think everyone deserves that. Already I hate this terrible war! May God be good to you."

"Remember meeeee," he called in a fading voice. And Hanna, pushing with all her might, burst out of the empty grave.

FOUR

Luckily for Hanna, the rain was over and a thick mist had rolled down the hill into the graveyard, hiding her as she rose from the shallow grave. Not ten feet from where she crouched, two gravediggers paused beside a donkey cart to toss in their shovels and light their pipes.

Ducking low, she forced herself to wait until they trudged past her, talking wearily about the burials to come in the morning. As soon as she could crawl out, Hanna covered the grave again. Now she was free to go after Mama.

The gray form of the hotel's carriage house loomed ahead. It had been enlarged because of the many ambulance horses that had to be stabled there now. From all the whinnying, Hanna sensed that someone was very late in throwing them their afternoon hay.

The sight of that place made Hanna think of her beloved Johnny Appleseed. If only Mama hadn't given him away to that farmer in Kentucky! She fell into a daydream as she hurried by. Johnny Appleseed was no ordinary horse. Most of them were so unemotional, but not him! No, he pined and pined, just like a dog. And one day when he couldn't stay away any longer, he'd taken a flying run over that farmer's rail fence, scrambled down to the great Ohio, swum all the way across it, and come galloping back home!

Hanna was a good distance past the stable when she heard someone shout, "Settle down, you danged horse!" Behind her, a rearing stallion pawed the air, trying to break free of the stablehand tugging at him with a rope. As she glanced over her shoulder, the huge animal lunged forward, kicked up its heels, reared back again, and twisted in midair. The lead line tore out of the man's hands, and the freed horse charged straight at Hanna.

Hanna was ready to spring away—until she saw the white diamond on his black muzzle. In those first galloping half-seconds, he seemed no older than when last she'd seen him years ago. It couldn't be him! And yet . . .

He stopped short, then walked up to Hanna and nuzzled her face. He nipped playfully at her shoulder in the way that only her Johnny Appleseed had ever done.

"Oh, you did come back! You did! You did!" Hanna began to cry. She hugged the old horse, letting her fingers curl through his thick black mane.

The stablehand had been shouting for the soldiers on guard duty to stop the thief. One of them came toward her now, unslinging the musket on his shoulder.

Hanna remembered what Papa had trained her to do when she was too small to lift a leg into a stirrup. Quickly stepping in front of Johnny Appleseed, she pressed the flat of a hand against the white diamond on his face. "Down," she said. As he obeyed, Hanna flung herself onto his back and over his neck, seizing his mane in both hands. "Go! Go! Go!"

Up sprang Johnny Appleseed, while cries of "Halt or I'll shoot!" rang out.

Hanna could have taken a chance on a wild downhill dash for the trees. Instead she wheeled the horse around and sent him galloping right past the leveled gun. "Can't you see this is my *own* horse? I'm no thief!" she screamed as they thundered by.

The startled soldier swung around, watching her go for a moment. Then he squeezed the trigger. But perhaps he had no real intention of hitting this pretty girl desperately clinging to the neck of an unsaddled horse. His bullet crashed harmlessly into an overhead branch.

There were no longer any overturned wagons to block their way down to the road. Hanna hiked up her long skirt and dropped her legs on both sides of Johnny Appleseed. He bounded down the road.

It was several pounding miles before the gallant stallion's true age began to show. He got overheated and tired, and Hanna climbed off to let him walk. She removed the rope that was still around his neck, tied a loop, and laid part of it across the inside of his mouth and the rest over his neck.

"Well, I've got reins, at least," she said, getting back on.

Hanna's heart began to pound as they drew near the river about a half hour after sunset. Already she could see flowing water through the trees. She came around the next bend in the road and got a clear view of the landing. But nothing was there except an old man sitting on a barrel, fishing.

"Mister," she called, riding up to him. "Can you tell me when the navy barge left?"

He gave her an annoyed look. "Don't you know better than to trot a horse on wooden planks when a man is a-settin' there with a rod in his hand? That racket's scaring off my fish."

"I'm sorry," she said.

"Oh, well," he sighed. "They don't do much bitin' around this time anyways. When did it leave? Can't tell you for a fact 'cause there wasn't anything here when I came down. But I did hear a horn blow, let's see, maybe three hours ago. That was most likely when the tug went off with the barge."

Three hours! Could she ride along the shore, overtake a tug with a three-hour lead, and swim Johnny Appleseed out to it? Hanna didn't know, but one thing was certain. No matter what she had to do so Mama could see with her own eyes and feel with her own hands that she was alive, Hanna was going to do it!

But what about *Rafe!*

It was only then that she became aware of distant singing. From somewhere up beyond the houses lining Hill Street a woman's full and powerful voice soared above the rest:

Go down, Moses
Way down in Egypt land
Tell ol' Pharaoh
Let my people go!

"If you're a-wondering what's going on," said the fisherman, shaking his head sadly, "the colored folks are a-havin' a hallelujah meeting over by the jailhouse. Those poor souls are taking their lives in their hands tryin' to get one of their own set free, and you don't want to be caught in the middle. Me neither. That's why I'm here, mindin' my own business."

"Well, maybe it *is* your business!" cried Hanna, wheeling Johnny Appleseed toward the street and galloping away.

As they reached the top of the hill, Hanna saw a crowd of white men rush into a tavern and hurry out again with jugs and bottles in each hand. Rosalie had called that tavern a hangout for the worst kind of trash. "They is the ones," she said, "that kin look halfway tall only when they're a-standin' on somebody else's face."

Now a man lurched up beside her, holding an empty bottle by the neck. "Here's one for you. Take it and bean a nigger."

Hanna took it. "I'd rather bean you!" she cried flinging it to the ground. "Only hitting you on the head wouldn't do any good!"

Other men were rushing toward the jail, clutching bottles or scooping up stones from garden walks. Hanna glanced at the windows and saw, by the light of candles, worried people moving back, curtains being drawn, frightened children in bedclothes clutching each other.

She heard the crash of glass farther on and the cries of people who'd been hit. And miracle of miracles, she still heard a wondrous voice singing. Now it was:

Oh-oh, Freedom!
Oh-oh, Freedom!
Oh-oh, Freedom over me-e-e!
And before I'll be a slave
I'll be buried in my grave
And go home to my Lord and be free!

No more cryin'
No more cryin'
No more cryin' over me-e-e
And before I'll be a slave—

With so much cursing, shouting, and missile throwing going on ahead, Hanna feared that Johnny Appleseed would spook. But he'd been in danger too many times with Mama and Rosalie to shy away now. Anna bent over his neck, urging him on. Like a bull with lowered horns, the galloping animal charged into the midst of the yowling mob. As they scattered in all directions, Hanna pulled up in front of the deacon's haywagon, behind which some of the protesters had crouched. Others stood their ground, holding bales of hay in front of them as shields. All were singing.

The shock of her coming through could not stop the rowdies for long. But there were others on the street. Some were recovering soldiers who'd not yet been sent back to their units. Some were townspeople who'd looked on at first in horror. One man came out of his front door with a shotgun. He fired it into the air, crying, "I can't believe this! Is this the United States of America? What in all getout are we sending our sons into battle for if this can go on right here in our own town? Why can't things just be as they were before?"

"I shall tell you why, sir," called the deacon, spitting blood that had run down to his mouth from a cut on his forehead. Risking still greater injury, he climbed up on top of the wagon. "It's because things as they were are full of injustice."

"That's right," declared one of the soldiers. "Mr. Lincoln said that a house divided against itself cannot stand. It is a sickness upon the soul to keep other men in bondage. That's why I went into this war."

"Then, you, soldier," cried someone from the mob, "are a nigger lover!"

"What I am is a *freedom* lover, and a lover of justice."

"As am I," called a woman from a window.

"And I!" said a man from the seat of his still-rolling carriage. "Has anyone been hurt?"

"Lookee here, boys!" called one of the drunks. "It's that doc who's so ugly he had to hitch himself up to an Injun squaw."

"That squaw, as you call her, Will Drover, picked you out of a gutter where you were drunk and had a knife in your side. Running Deer took care of your eldest girl after you nearly beat her to death because she wouldn't marry the preacher who'd caught you robbing his collection box. And she helped me care for your poor suffering wife during the last days of her illness. May God take better care of her in heaven than you ever bothered to. And as for the rest of you ruffians, the next one who dares to throw anything at these people had better watch out. I will personally go to the sheriff and swear out a warrant."

"The sheriff won't do nothing," growled someone from the shadows.

"Then lawyer Abercrombie and I will go directly to the judge in the courthouse. And if that doesn't work, I will write to the governor and to General Ulysses Grant about what a nest of treason there is here on this side of the Ohio."

"Hold on now," called an onlooker who'd taken no part in the mob. "I'm as much in favor of fighting to keep the Union together as anyone. But this is a white country for the white race. Even President Lincoln himself never said that the coloreds are equal to whites."

"If that's so, it's only because he don't know us yet!" called a young man with the end of a broken bone sticking out of his leg. Coming out from behind the haywagon, he dragged that leg to the jailhouse door.

"Deputy Stokes!" he cried, banging hard. "We are done praying. Now we're saying, no more of being beaten and burned and carried away in chains! We will do whatever it takes to stop it. And in this town that means we're talking straight to you, O high and mighty Knight of the Golden Jackasses! You take your bloody hands off our brother in there and you keep them to yourself. Do you hear?"

In the dead silence that followed, a voice inside said very calmly, "Oh, yeah, I hear. I hear real good. More important than that, boy, I even know who you are an' where you live. But, heck, don't let that scare you none. You just wait for me right there."

Hanna saw the young man flinch, but he held his ground as the door was slowly unlocked from inside and swung open.

The leader of the murderous Knights of the Golden Circle stepped out with his hands in his pockets. "See where my hands are?" he said. Hanna thought that the easygoing smile on his face as he strolled into the center of the vigil keepers made him seem even more dangerous. "Now all this here noise puts a man out of sorts. But I aim to please. Is there anything I can do for anybody?"

"Yes," cried Hanna, glaring straight at him. "We want to see Rafe Sims right now."

"Why, Miss Bowes," he said, grinning, "you can see him down at your daddy's plantation. An agent from the Owner's Association came by for him not more 'n an hour after you left here. He had all the legal papers, so naturally I had to turn the boy over. They took the ferry back to Kentucky, I do believe, and they're long gone now. Anybody who wants to call me a liar is welcome to look." His big hands came out of his pockets, and he cracked his knuckles loud enough for all to hear.

For a moment there was only stillness. Then the young man who had banged on the door started to limp through it. Several others rushed to join him, including one of the soldiers. But Hanna hadn't moved. She was staring hard at the deputy, watching the look of triumph and satisfaction rising on his face. When the vigil keepers came out shaking their heads in sorrow, the mob broke into cheers.

"For shame, you rock-throwing cowards!" an old white lady cried out at them. "How can anybody rejoice that another one of God's children has been dragged away in chains?"

"That's telling us, Widow Greer," one of the drunks called back at her, laughing. Then he walked away with his friends, still chuckling over the big joke that was played on the "uppity niggers."

61

There were other white townspeople who had kept their distance while dangerous objects were flying. But now, for the first time in their lives, some went up to shake the hands of black townspeople and say how badly they felt. Doctor Vickers had been busy all along, treating cuts with the ointments in his black bag. But it was the fellow with the broken leg who needed the most tending, and as soon as the young man had been carefully set down in the carriage, the doctor drove off with him. The deacon asked all the brothers and sisters who'd fit to climb onto the haywagon, and the rest to walk close beside it as they went back through town. It would be best, he said, for everybody to stay together that night, and for those who knew how to shoot to take turns standing guard with the one shotgun they had among them.

Everyone wanted Hanna to come along. Johnny Appleseed didn't wait for his own invitation. The big horse had been pulling mouthfuls of hay from the wagon, and he wasn't about to let the wagon leave without him. But Hanna held him back. No tears had flowed from her eyes yet. There would be time enough for that later. Right now she had to go after Rafe!

FIVE

Johnny Appleseed galloped down to the river. But the closer he came to the small ferry dock, the slower he went. It was from here that Mama and Rosalie would so often cross over into slave country on missions for the Underground Railroad. And horses will remember places where their masters gave off the powerful scent of fear.

But he needn't have been troubled—the big log raft with the long oar at the stern wasn't there. Peering into the darkness, Hanna saw nothing. Listening, she heard not a splash.

Hanna dismounted to let Johnny Appleseed graze on the few tufts of grass poking up along the shore. Meanwhile she tried to control her jumpiness. Yet how could she when she had no way of knowing when the ferryman was coming back—or even whether it would be tonight at all?

As the time dragged on, fretful pictures came into her mind: the Squire hanging Rafe from a tree as a lesson to his other slaves; Rosalie, with her bad heart condition, learning what had happened to her son; Mom and Dad and Kevin searching the house for her.

She was still lost in her thoughts when Johnny Appleseed's long neck lifted up, and a fluttering sound came from his mouth. It was only then that Hanna noticed the dark shape of a powerfully built man floating toward her. His raft hit the dock with a dull thud, and she hurried toward him.

"Excuse me," Hanna said anxiously, as he looped a rope around a post and stepped off. "I know it's late, but could you please take me to the other side now? I can't tell you how terribly important it is."

"Never forget a face," he declared, looking straight past her at Johnny Appleseed. "That danged horse is a misery to get on and a stomper when he *is* on. Not to mention that the current tonight is so danged bad, I cain't hardly straighten out my back." Leaving her standing there, he headed for a tarpaper and clapboard shack nearby.

"The morning might be too late! Won't you please help me?"

"Well, now, that depends," he called back over his shoulder. "How much are ye fixin' to pay me?"

"Two dollars."

"Haw! Them's my *daytime* rates, so ferget it." He opened the door.

"But it's all I have! Look, I'll get you more when I come back, I promise!"

He paused for a minute. "Lemme see if you even got that much."

Hanna rushed up, thanking him as she opened the purse and poured the coins into his outstretched hand.

Counting carefully, he stuffed them in a pocket. "Well, I see that ye do. And like I said afore, if ye come back tomorrow, I'll take ye. That's providin' my back is better.

Now don't think I don't know what is so all-fired important that you got ter be chasing over in the night. I know whose carriage horse that is. And I remember the colored woman who used to come riding along and stuck a pistol in my gut one time when I looked too close at what was being hid inside her carriage. Now I'm watchin' you. So you git!"

Hanna did "git," but not very far. Leading Johnny Appleseed down the road until they were out of sight, she hitched him loosely to a tree, then circled back to the dock in a low crouch. Careful to make no noise, she settled down behind a briar patch to stare down at the window at the rear of the shack. A single lantern glowed from its place near the window. Hanna watched the ferryman throw off his shirt and start to rub his sore muscles. Eventually, he stretched and tilted back his head. So thin were those walls that Hanna could hear his yawn. Then, all at once, he dropped out of sight.

As soon as she heard snoring, Hanna hurried back to her horse, sat down on the ground, and pulled off her petticoat. If only she had *scissors!* Well, her teeth and a sharp rock would have to do. After a lot of yanking and tearing, Hanna had four strips of cloth. She wrapped them around Johnny Appleseed's hoofs.

Walking carefully herself, she led him back to the dock. Guiding Johnny Appleseed one leg at a time, she brought him to the edge of the raft. But he was already breathing heavily, his nostrils flaring. That thing before him bobbing on the water was making him go bug-eyed.

"Now you listen to me," Hanna whispered furiously into

his perked-up ear. "If you dare to make any more fuss about this, I'll never take you anywhere again!"

Those words may have had no meaning for Johnny Appleseed, but he certainly understood the way she'd said them. He took one hesitant step upon the ferry. And then, with a growing pride and self-confidence, he simply climbed aboard.

Hanna lost no time lifting the tie rope from its post and pushing off with her feet. The flat boat slipped easily away from the dock. As it began to drift, she went to the huge oar that served as both a rudder for steering and a paddle for pushing. Her first task was to swing the ferry around to face the Kentucky shore. But it took the thick arms and shoulders of a ferryman plus a good deal of skill to handle this oar just right. The next thing she knew, the craft was spinning.

Johnny Appleseed snorted, and no amount of covering on his hoofs could stop him from stomping. These sounds carried loudly over water—loudly enough to reach the tarpaper shack. The ferryman's door flew open and he heaved himself out, bellowing curses and belching fire from his shotgun. The horse reared. Hanna ducked. If it hadn't been for that powerful current the ferryman had complained about, they might still have been within shooting range.

As the current swept the raft quickly downriver, Hanna went back to the work of getting control of the steering. Her efforts got the raft out to the middle of the stream, but by then exhaustion made her sink to her knees with her arms around the oar. How sleepy she suddenly felt. When had she last closed her eyes? Why, twenty-four hours ago at least!

"No wonder I'm so pooped," she would have said had she still felt like Anna Post. But something changes in a person when she jumps a century and a half back in time. With every passing minute she was becoming more fully Hanna. Those years she had spent in the future seemed to be slipping away from her. Or was it just from exhaustion that the faces of Mom and Dad and Kevin were growing so blurry in her memory?

"But I can't let myself forget them!" she cried aloud. And her eyes, which had been closing all the while, popped wide open. "I can't."

Johnny Appleseed, stepping very gingerly on the raft, came over to nuzzle her. "Oh, you don't need me to forgive you," she said, when he kept pressing his muzzle against her. "None of this is your fault. Now, I want you to be real good and don't rock this thing while I just set myself down to rest a spell. All right?"

Telling herself it would only be for a minute or two, Hanna shut her eyes. But even before she sank back and rolled over on her side, she had fallen dead asleep.

Hanna awoke to sunbeams dancing on her eyelids and the sweet smell of earth and flowers in her nose. A big monarch butterfly flitted past her face, and she sat up, shading her eyes. The raft had run aground. Johnny Appleseed's hoofprints could be seen in the soft mud going up the gentle slope. Farther along, beyond a patch of huckleberry bushes, Hanna saw him munching away in a field of sky-blue cornflowers and pink clover.

She was hungry herself, and thirsty as well. But the river water looked too mucky to gulp. Climbing the slope, she found that almost all the berries were dried up or gone, maybe pecked at by birds. But farther back, beyond the briars and the flowers, acres of farmland stretched before her.

Hanna followed a dirt track through the fields and picked tomatoes, peas, and ears of corn, so sweet and delicious bitten into raw. She and Johnny Appleseed came to a clear stream from which they both drank. Then she mounted up and rode to the nearest farmhouse.

Not far from the barn, a boy sat on a log whittling a thick piece of wood. There was a big white stain all around his mouth and a milk bucket near his feet.

"How do," she said politely.

"Sometimes I do fine, sometimes I do better," he replied, looking up slowly but giving almost all of his attention to Johnny Appleseed. "Don't you know better then to pull on a horse's mouth with rope bristles? That's got to hurt something awful."

"Oh, you must be right! But I just didn't have anything else."

"So what? That ain't the horse's fault. What's his name?"

"Johnny Appleseed."

"You see that apple orchard back yonder near the woods? It were the *real* Johnny Appleseed who come down from the Ohio Valley with a bag o' seeds and started it for my grandpa."

"Get out."

"It's true!"

"Fancy that." Her gaze dropped to the creamy white pail. "That must be good milk. You sure seem to have enjoyed it."

"It's even better buttermilk," he said, licking his lips and grinning at her.

Hanna raised an eyebrow. "Now you're going to tell me you've got a cow that gives buttermilk."

"You wanna bet me your horse that this here ain't buttermilk?"

"Well, no. But I'd sure like to find out fer myself."

"Whyn't you just say you want some?"

"All right, I want some."

"What're you gonna trade fer it?"

"Don't have anything to trade with."

"What about that purse?"

"There's nothing in it."

"That's all right. I'll give it to my ma."

"All right."

As she started to take it off, the door banged open and a round little woman stepped out, calling, "Aaron, you'll do no sech a thang as take any of that poor girl's belongings. You give her some of that buttermilk right now."

"I was gonna give her a bridle too, Ma, only it were a surprise."

"Well, you surely will give her the bridle. But you don't take anything. Here's a clean mug fer her too. And you wipe off your face and stand up when you talk to a young lady. I want to see some good manners round here."

"I was going to give you a bridle," Aaron told Hanna in a low, mopey voice as he dipped the mug into the pail.

"Kevin," she muttered, climbing down for it.

"What?"

"Nothin'. You reminded me of someone." Hanna took a long drink of buttermilk. "Why, it's been ever so long since I tasted anything as good as this! A hundred and fifty years at least!"

Aaron stared at her. "You talk funny."

"Oh? How so?"

"Dunno. Most girls only bill and coo like this when they're a-trying to git themselves married."

"*Married?* I should think not!"

"Say, don't get mad at *me*. I wouldn't marry you on a bet. Wouldn't marry anybody. Soon as I'm growed up I'm heading west!"

"Don't you be a-listenin' to him," called his mother, appearing at the door again. This time she had an apron on. "You had your breakfast yet? I got the bacon on already. Iffen you like that buttermilk, you'll just die over my flapjacks!"

"I'm sure I would, ma'am, and I thank you so kindly, but I'm in a terrible hurry to get to Bowesboro. Do you know where it is?"

"Don't think I ever heard of it. Kin you tell me what it's near?"

"Near? Well, I don't have any . . . Wait, yes, I do. It's a few hours ride from the plantation at Fairweather Valley."

"Then you might could go down the road 'bout two mile and ask Isaiah Fairweather about it."

"Someone from the *family?*" cried Hanna excitedly.

"Well, I 'spect he took the name like slaves sometimes do.

He used to be a house slave there before his mistress died."

"That was my mama's Aunt Ida."

"Oh," said the woman, and her face fell.

Hanna grew uncomfortable. "She promised my mama to set the slaves free."

"If what you mean by free is that a blind old man with arthritis was thrown out of his home to feed and care for hisself, then I suppose you might say he's free."

"Uh . . . how will I recognize . . . ?"

"It's a closed-down sawmill," the woman replied coldly. "Be keerful of the rotting old wood laying around so you don't step on a snake. How he keeps away from them, I don't know." She fell silent for a moment and asked, "So how do you feel about slavery?"

"With all my heart and soul I hate it!"

"So do I, " said the woman, brightening again. "Long as you're goin' over t' his place, maybe you wouldn't mind taking him some of my fresh baked cornbread an' a few other things?"

"I'd be so happy to."

"Then you wait right here," she said, heading back into the house. "Aaron, go and fetch her your grandpa's Mexico saddle."

"All right, Ma. But the mice have been at the leather mighty fierce."

"Just as long as the straps ain't bit through. Brang it out anyways, son."

"Yes'm." He headed for the barn and returned with a bridle between his teeth and carrying a carved wood and brass-studded saddle that was almost as large as he was. Hanna led Johnny Appleseed to him, and he tossed the saddle over the horse's middle.

Hanna, meanwhile, went in front with the bridle and removed the rope. "Oh, Johnny Appleseed, your poor mouth *is* sore!"

"That's what I told you!" the boy declared. He began pulling the saddle straps tight and would not allow her to help.

Hanna felt uncomfortable about taking these gifts. When Aaron's mother came out, she protested, "But don't you need this saddle and bridle for yourselves?"

"No, not at all. Mostly we use our horse to pull the plow or carry thangs. And when we go out on a Sunday, he's hitched to the buckboard."

"Well, I don't know how to thank you fer being so gen'rus," Hanna said. She put one foot into the stirrup, lifted herself up, and reached for the sack of food. "Who should I tell him sent these?"

"Oh, we all try to be good neighbors here. It don't matter who."

"The name is Lamb," Aaron piped up.

"And you *are* a lamb!" declared Hanna, settling into the saddle. "Thank you so much for everything. Bless you both!"

They waved to her as she left. Just before Hanna sent Johnny Appleseed into a canter, she called back, "I can't ever recall such marvelous buttermilk!"

As Hanna rode along, she tried to remember which of Aunt Ida's house servants at Fairweather Hall was Isaiah.

Wasn't he that tall, gray-haired man Mama wouldn't allow to carry me up the steps after I'd taken a fever on the way there? she asked herself.

"I'm truly glad to see you," Mama had told him, "but I cannot be against slavery and make use of it at the same time."

The issue of slavery had kept Mama and her aunt separated from each other for nine years. But there they were, together at last, arguing and crying and hugging and kissing all at the same time. They'd laid Hanna down in a big brass bed and climbed in themselves on either side of her to talk the night away. It was to the sound of their voices and the feel of their arms about her that Hanna had drifted out of her fever and the dreadful fears that had brought it on.

Her daydreaming came to an end at the messy clearing in front of the ruined sawmill. The big building, which was set farther back, had long ago burned down, and what remained of its timbers were charred as black as coal. But a shed with a tin roof was still standing to one side of it. Once it had been used for storing tools. Now, though, those tools were rusting in a heap outside, and a stovepipe sticking out of an opening in one wall was giving off smoke.

When Hanna gave Johnny Appleseed a gentle nudge to turn in there, he obeyed. But his tossing head told what he really felt about having to pass between those piles of decaying logs and broken boards.

Looking around, Hanna could see nothing dangerous, nothing about to strike. Just in case he was getting ready to bolt, however, she got down to lead him by the bridle.

"Now, aren't you too big to be such a scaredy-cat?" Hanna murmured. Stepping pretty carefully herself, she led him to the shed. Through the open door she heard puttering, and she called, "Mr. Fairweather?"

"Dear me, I have a visitor, and I'm not sure I know that voice. Please forgive me if I don't ask you to come inside," he called back in a soft, elderly voice.

"That's all right."

"It's these eyes of mine, you see. There is a dark cloud in front of them, and it's only where the light is very bright that I can make out anything at all. Do sit yourself down at that little table outside and I'll be right along. If you wouldn't mind sitting in the sunlight, then you'll be darker than my cloud, and I can look at that shadow. Do you fancy a cup of tea?"

"Yes, please, that would be nice."

"Good, good. But you must be prepared for an unusual taste. It will be good for you, though, I promise. I don't often allow myself to make this particular brew, there is so little of it left. The mistress bought a packet of it in Indiana from someone who knew the remedies of the forest. After she died no one wanted it but me. Well, it didn't help my failing eyesight much, but it certainly has been a kindness to these creaky bones. There now, the pot is ready. "

"Someone in Indiana who knew the remedies of the forest," Hanna repeated to herself. Her mouth dropped open. "Mr. Fairweather, do you know if it was bought from a person called the Conjure Woman?"

"Why, yes, I believe so," he said excitedly. "Oh, you must

74

tell me who you are." Two cups rattled on a tray as he emerged, looking old and bent but still as dignified as ever.

"I'm Hanna Terwilliger. My mother is Aunt Ida's niece, Dora!"

"This is very confusing to me." He put down the tray and felt for the empty chair. "I understood that the child, Hanna, disappeared many years ago and has never been found."

"Yes, that's true. But I wasn't *killed*. I didn't *die*. Something happened to me that sent me to another place. I know it's very hard to explain or believe, but I came back! Only the hotel's a hospital now. Papa's away in the army, and Mama just left to take some wagons full of medicine down to the soldiers who are fighting in Tennessee. I'm going after her to show her I'm all right. Only there's something very important I have to do first!"

Hanna blurted all this at him in a thundering rush. The old man was clearly bewildered. "You must forgive me if I'm a little slow," he said as he leaned across the table. "If only I could see your face."

"We came to cousin Amanda's wedding. I wasn't feeling well, but Mama wouldn't let you take me from her."

"Why, yes. *Yes!* Oh, my. It *is* you. Such good and wonderful news!"

"Thank you," said Hanna, growing teary-eyed. "I'm very proud that you chose the name of Fairweather."

At this he drew back from her. "I must tell you that the name was always mine by rights," he said stiffly.

What had just gone wrong? "I . . . I don't understand."

"No, I suppose not." He fell silent, and she waited. Finally, he said, "Perhaps I should have given you something sweet to put in your tea. Have you tasted it yet?"

"No, I will." She took a sip. "It's very good."

"I should not have said anything, I suppose," he sighed.

She brought the cup down so hard on the table that it almost broke. "Yes, you should!"

"Well, then, how do I put this?" he asked himself. "Ida and I had different mothers. Our father, though, was the same man, a white man—your grandfather, Adam Fairweather."

Hanna jumped to her feet. "You're Aunt Ida's *brother?*"

"I am indeed. Her half-brother."

"But . . . but . . . then how could she have treated you as a slave?"

"That is what I was. When the mother is a slave, then the child is a slave."

"But didn't she know she was your sister?"

"Your mother's aunt had many good qualities. But there were certain matters she did not allow herself to think about. More to the point, neither did my father. From earliest childhood, he trained her to see what she should see and *not* see what she shouldn't see, if you know what I mean."

"You're my uncle then."

"Your grand-uncle, yes."

"Oh!" She rushed over to embrace him.

"Why, your face is wet. You're crying. I am very moved, but no, you mustn't."

"Uncle Isaiah, I don't want you to live by yourself

anymore. Promise me that as soon as I'm finished with . . . with what I have to do you'll come back home with me."

"Oh, I'm doing very well here."

"But you can hardly see!"

"Would I see much better in Indiana?"

She stepped back. "Why are you making things so difficult?"

"Only a free person," he said with a smile, "can make things difficult. Are you even certain I'll be wanted?"

"You don't know my mama if you have to ask that!"

"Oh yes, I do know your mother. I helped look after her for more than twenty years."

"Didn't she know you were her uncle?"

"Your mother's nurse, who loved her so, came very close to telling little Dora once. That is why your grandfather got rid of her. He sold her off, and it broke your mother's heart. Mine too. She was my first wife, but I never learned where she was sent. Nor our own little child either." He had lowered his head, but Hanna could still see a trembling cheek.

They sat together in silence. "Do you know where I can get a gun?" Hanna asked at last.

"A gun! Why would you need such a thing?"

Hanna told him about Rafe and what she hoped to do. Isaiah remained silent for a long time after she finished. "I wish you would not take such a risk when your chances are so very small."

"Uncle Isaiah, I have to try! I need a gun and I need you to tell me, if you can, how to get to Bowesboro."

When nothing he could say would make her change her mind, the old man went into the shed. He came out again with an old, long-barreled horse pistol a neighbor had given him to shoot at any snakes he might hear in the woodpiles.

"I've never used it anyway," he told her. "The snakes don't find me very interesting, and there is just too much that has to be done to load it."

"Papa taught me how to pour in the firing powder and put in the wad and drop the ball on top of that and—"

"I believe you." He handed Hanna the ammunition pouch and the ramrod that went with it. "I'll wager it was your mother, though, who taught you how to shoot."

"No, Papa did. But he said I have her natural aim!"

After giving her directions to Bowesboro, Isaiah added, "Don't go straight to the plantation. Go around behind it and come in through the fields. Cover yourself first with as much mud as you can. It won't stop any hound dogs from finding you, but they won't smell your fear as much. Stand still if they come at you and they just might leave you alone."

"How do you know all this?"

"Oh," he said, "once I went looking for my wife."

"What happened?"

He shook his head and would say nothing more about it. It wasn't until Hanna was ready to leave that she remembered to give him Mrs. Lamb's best wishes and her gifts. Then she asked him one more question. "I don't remember you speaking this well when I first met you. Could you do it then?"

He smiled and said, "What is your best guess?"

"I think you must have taught yourself to read and write."

"That's true."

"But you did it in secret?"

"Also true. Otherwise it would have made some people very uncomfortable."

"Including Aunt Ida and Mama?"

He only smiled. "Good luck, dear Hanna. How I wish I could see your face just this once."

"But I can see yours!" she said, and they embraced one last time before she left.

Hanna had already traveled some of the distance to Bowesboro while sleeping on the drifting ferry, but many hours of riding and walking still lay ahead. The narrow dirt road she was on twisted up and up through woody hills. The farms grew fewer, and those she did pass were scraggly and rocky and seemed to be growing more children than crops. The very young children played naked in the sun while older boys and girls went about in rags chopping wood, hauling water, or bending over in the fields beside their fathers.

Whatever their ages or sizes, the children stopped what they were doing when she went by. To Hanna, it seemed as if her having a horse and saddle made her a princess in a fairy tale.

Hanna had the road to herself for hours at a time. Once in a while, she'd meet a farmer driving a buckboard and have to move to the side to let it pass. At one point a whole family came along in one, and when they all smiled at her, she stopped and asked how far it was to the pike.

"Where are you heading, dear?" the wife asked.

"Bowesboro."

"Well, then, you're a-goin' the long way," declared her husband. "They's a loggin' road up ahead 'bout four miles or so. Iffen ye don't mind a-watchin' out fer a mountain lion or a bear now and then, you're gonna save a lot of time. Otherwise, you're a-goin' to be campin' out on the road tonight. An' I 'spect they's goin' to be a humdinger of a storm."

"Why, that's a fearsome place to be a-sendin' this girl, Mr. Snodgrass," said the man's wife. "First of all, that's only a trail and easy to get lost on. Second of all, they's all manner of other dang'rus animals up there. Why, just the screamin' of them bobcats and panthers will send the hair a-flyin' straight up from your scalp!"

"Now, now, Mrs. Snodgrass," said her husband, "ain't a scream in the world ever hurt anyone, 'specially daytimes. And mostly them wild critters will leave a body alone."

"*Mostly*, Mr. Snodgrass, ain't *always*."

"Well, nuthin' ain't always. All she has to do is stay to the right when the trail forks near the top, and it'll take her straight down to the pike on the other side."

"Maybe you ain't taken a real good look at this girl in them long clothes and everythang. She is refined. Cain't you see she don't know the way of the woods?"

"Oh, I reckon I do know some of it, ma'am," said Hanna in her country voice. "But I thank you both kindly for tellin' me the one way or t'other of it."

"Why, you're most welcome, I'm sure," they answered together.

Till now the children, three little girls and all very shy, had said nothing. Now the oldest tugged at her mother's arm and whispered, "Ask Pa to tell her about the suspicious man back thar."

"Oh, that's a good idea. The man with the stovepipe hat, Mr. Snodgrass. She being all alone, you know."

"Yes, I think so. Missy, there's a feller we passed restin' up his horse. It's all lathered up and he don't look too good hisself."

"He don't seem to us a right Christian, dear. Bad look in his eye," Mrs. Snodgrass added.

"I'll watch out," Hanna said. Thanking them again, she rode off, preparing the horse pistol.

SIX

Hanna hadn't gotten far before she spotted the suspicious man in the stovepipe hat the Snodgrass family had warned her about. He was coming along slowly on his horse. Even from a distance she could see that he was dirty and scruffy, probably smelly too. There was a cockeyed look on his face that made her hope he was more drunk than dangerous. But when he looked behind him to see if anyone else was coming, Hanna dropped her right hand into the saddlebag and wrapped it around the gun handle.

He made a sudden movement, but it was only to sweep off his hat like a polite gentleman. That just made him seem all the more menacing. "Allow me to beg your pardon for speaking to a young lady before I'm spoken to," he said in a phony-sounding voice. "But don't you know that you shouldn't be out here on the open road all alone?"

"Oh, I've got company," Hanna said evenly, though her heart was pumping harder than a steam engine. She took out the gun and placed it across the front of her saddle. That way, she could hold it steady even if her hand shook.

The sight of an ancient horse pistol only made the man grin. He planted the hat back on his head, freeing his hands. "All primed and ready for action, is it?"

Hanna forced herself to meet his gaze. "Somebody might find that out."

"Well, good for you! There are so many bad characters on the road these days. That's why I keep this fifteen shot Henry carbine, all loaded up with the hammer cocked. Took it off a dead cavalryman down east of Memphis. Must be worth at least a hundred dollars. You want to buy it?" He drew it out and laid it across an arm.

"I don't have any money."

"Aw, come on now. A young lady traveling all by herself and she don't carry any money? Why, that's a scandal." His tone grew dark. "I don't believe you."

Hanna pointed the single shot horse pistol directly at his middle. "You're thinking I might not shoot you, but I will."

"You go ahead then!" he shouted and stuck his chest out. "Go first, why don't you? You'll see I'm not scared of dying." He closed his eyes, and suddenly he looked very young. Young, yes, and trembling.

Hanna lowered her pistol. "What's going on here?" she said, as much to herself as to him.

"They don't give a fellow a chance to make up his own mind about going into a battle!" he cried. "They just send him into it with the cannons banging and the rebels screaming how they're going to cut you to pieces. And they come galloping at you through the smoke with their eyes so bloodshot, it's like they're fresh out of hell, and their bayonets are pointing straight at your heart! You don't get no chance to set your mind on just being brave when your horse turns right around under you. And you know the general's going to call you a coward and a deserter and make an example of you, which isn't fair because you're not! It's just that you weren't set in your mind for it so soon. But by then, it's too late, you see? Everybody's lying dead behind you and you're running!"

"How old are you?" Hanna asked gently.

"Sixteen."

"Did they let you in so young?"

He shook his head. "The recruiting sergeants don't care if you lie about your age."

"Did you give your right name?"

"No, I couldn't do that. My folks would have found out."

"So you didn't join up near where you live?"

"Couldn't. My folks would have stopped me certain."

"Then nobody in the army knows who you really are."

"Yes, but *I* know!"

"But you could join up again, couldn't you?" Hanna suggested. "I mean, just wait until you're a little older, and if that's what you still want . . ."

"So you don't think I'm a coward?"

"How could I when you were just daring me to shoot you?"

"Oh, I knew you wouldn't."

"How can you be so sure?"

He grinned. "You didn't cock the pistol."

"Take another look."

The boy's smile faded. "But you see, I didn't know that!"

"You took a chance though."

"That's true."

"Can I have a look at that carbine?"

"All right," he said, handing it over. "But be careful with it."

"How do you fire those fifteen shots, just hold the trigger down after the first goes off?"

He laughed at her foolishness. "Why, no, who ever heard of such a thing? What you do is you pull that lever behind the hammer each time."

"You mean by putting my finger in this loop?"

"That's it. When you pull it down, it throws out the casing for the last bullet you fired. Then you push the lever up and another bullet goes into the chamber. It's real fast action, but I didn't get to use it."

"I'll tell you something," Hanna said when he put his hand out for the gun. "I don't think becoming an outlaw is the way to show yourself how brave you can be. I think going home is."

"Maybe so. I don't know yet. Can I have my carbine back?"

"No, you may not," she said, pulling at the reins to back Johnny Appleseed away from him. "You put me in fear for my life with this. So I think you owe it to me."

"Why, no, I don't! Here now, you better give it to me. That's mine." Standing up in his stirrups, he made a lunge for it.

"It the army's!" Hanna cried, backing all the way around him. "When I'm through with it, I'll return it to them."

"What are you going to do with a repeating rifle?" he said, chasing her in a circle.

"Maybe save somebody's life."

"But I could get real money for that piece."

"Look at it this way. If the army catches *you* with it, they'll make you say how you got it. Do you want to take a chance on that?"

"I want to make my own decision about it. Don't you trust me to make the right one?"

"Trust you? You tried to rob me!"

"Well, that's true, but now I know you better."

"Why did you join the army anyway?" Hanna asked. "Was it to save your country? Or to finish off slavery? Or because you wanted to be a hero?"

He stopped his horse. "I suppose it was to be a hero. What's wrong with that? That's why most fellers join up."

"It's the most stupid reason I can think of! No wonder you didn't stay with it. Go on home now."

"You're bossy as a schoolmarm, you know that?"

"Yes, I do. They say it's my best trait. Good-bye now, Jesse James."

"Who is Jesse James?"

"You'll hear of him someday. Bye now."

"Bye, you highway robber."

They rode off in opposite directions. It wasn't long before Hanna found the logging trail. As for wild animals, she saw neither hide nor hair of any during the long, hard trudge up the steep mountain. Her only problem was when small rocks were kicked out from under Johnny Appleseed's front hoofs and he'd start to slide. When they finally drew near the top, Hanna stopped to wipe the beads of sweat from her eyes and looked around for the spot where Mr. Snodgrass said the trail forked.

But it must have been a very long time since last he'd been up here. The trail itself had disappeared under a tangle of fallen branches and upturned tree trunks. She slid off Johnny Appleseed's back to take a look around. Stepping carefully, she climbed to the top of the mountain and scouted around until she found a path leading down the other side.

Johnny Appleseed, meanwhile, had scented something in the air that he did not like. He stomped and whinnied, and Hanna whirled around. "Wait! Wait! I'm coming for you!" she cried as she ran, worried he would break a leg in the tangled underbrush. But a fallen limb caught *her* ankle; she pitched forward and fell. By the time Hanna pushed herself up, the horse had bolted. She limped out of the tangle but couldn't see where he had gone.

Again and again she called out to him. It was only when she heard his snort and turned around that she saw him calmly standing on the crest of the mountain, waiting for her.

By the time they reached level ground in the next valley, Hanna heard the tramp of many hundreds of marching feet. Even before she got to the main road, she could make out the soldiers marching four abreast, rifles slung at their sides, food pans rattling on their belts, and heavy knapsacks on their backs. From the way many of them were muttering and coughing, it was clear they were miserable, choked with dust and very tired.

A sergeant moving more quickly than his men called out, "Step it up, Riley. Right, left, right, left! What's eating you? You don't like a little walk?"

"Oh, it's been a lovely stroll for sure, Sergeant. But now some of us would like to know when we might get back on the railroad again."

"Tell you what, soldier. You find us some part of the tracks that the raiders ain't torn up yet, and then you can snooze all the way down to Tennessee."

As Hanna came to the side of the road, an officer on horseback approached her, a wary look on his face. "Who are you?" he asked, squinting at her in the sun. "And why are you watching us? Counting numbers?"

"I'm just waiting to get on the road."

"So you can report to the Copperheads and they can report to the raiders?"

"No, sir. I'm loyal. My papa is a colonel in the army."

"What regiment?"

"I . . . don't know."

"That's surprising. What branch then? Infantry? Cavalry? Artillery?"

"I'm not sure."

When Johnny Appleseed shifted slightly, the major saw the stock of the carbine jutting from the saddlebag. As he started to pull it out, Hanna grabbed for it instinctively, but she let go under his angry gaze. "This is cavalry issue. Where did you get it?" he demanded.

"From a boy who was going home because he couldn't stand the fighting."

"A deserter."

"He was only sixteen. He didn't know what he was getting into."

The major sighed and turned to a young captain coming up. "Here, I'm sure you can use this."

"Thank you, sir."

He turned back to Hanna. "Do you have any papers that show who you are?"

"No."

Now he looked Johnny Appleseed over. "Where did you get this stallion? From that same deserter?"

Hanna stiffened. "I've had him all my life."

"We need horses," said the officer. "I'll give you twenty dollars for him."

"I won't sell him."

"This is wartime, Miss. We can simply take him."

"I need him myself," she suddenly blurted in a rush. "My mother runs a hospital for the Sanitary Commission, and—"

He gave her a disbelieving look. "A *woman* runs a hospital?"

"Yes, a *woman*. It's not a big place like the one in Mound City, but when they can't take all of the wounded that come up on the *Red Rover* steamboat, her hospital takes the rest. But now she's gone to the front with a bunch of wagons full of medical supplies. I got started late and I'm trying to catch up to her."

"You're a nurse?"

"Not yet, but I will be."

"You say your father's a colonel? What's his name?"

"Terwilliger."

"Never heard of him."

The captain chimed in. "Is that *Amos* Terwilliger?"

"Yes!" Hanna cried eagerly.

Lowering his voice as if to confide something shameful, he said, "Major, that's the officer who volunteered to train colored troops."

They both looked at her, and the major asked, "A family of abolitionists?"

"Yes, and proud of it."

"Well, I'm from one myself," he said with a smile. "I must say I admire what Colonel Terwilliger is doing. Tell you what. At the next break in the column, fall in. We will get you as far as Memphis a lot more safely."

"I really appreciate this, Major, but there's something I have to do first in Bowesboro. And besides that I can move much faster if I just go on ahead."

"No, I won't let you travel by yourself. This may be Union territory on paper and far behind the lines, but the truth is quite different. The rebels move among us like water passing through the fingers of your hand. At the very least they'll take your horse, and you could easily get shot in the bargain. Captain, you let me know if any of the men show her the slightest disrespect."

"Yes, sir."

He rode away from Hanna, calling out, "Sergeants, put some life into these soldiers!" From down the line someone began a marching song. Soon many of the young men singing it were looking at her.

Oh, how old are you, my purty little miss
How old are you, my honeeeey?
She answered me with a "Tee hee hee
I'll be sixteen next Sunday!"

Well, it's one more river I'm bound to cross
One more river I'm bound to cross
One more river I'm bound to cross
So ladies, fare thee well!

Well, I make my living in Sandy Land
I make my living in Sandy Land
I make my living in Sandy Land
And I'll marry you some day.

When the song came around again, Hanna chimed in:

Possum up a cinnamon tree
Raccoon in the larder
Any boy wants to marry me
Will have to try much harder!

Slow but safe. That's how it went until a lone sniper's bullet from a long Kentucky rifle on a hillside sent hundreds of soldiers running for cover or hitting the dirt.

It also made Johnny Appleseed very nervous. While Hanna stroked his neck, sergeants yelled at their frightened men to get up. "Why, this ain't nothing," one of them bellowed. "If you babies are scared over just one gunshot, what are you gonna do when we *really* get to the war?"

Two of the mounted officers had dashed into the trees with pistols drawn. They came back later, shaking their heads. The major gave a hand signal and the sergeants up and down the line barked, "Form up! Move out."

"You'd think we were in enemy territory," a private grumbled, dusting himself off.

"Who says we ain't?"

As the march began again, the captain rode up beside Hanna. "I never saw a female who looked so ready to fight like a soldier."

"What do you mean?"

"We took your carbine away. But when that sniper shot at us, you pulled a pistol. I thought nurses didn't carry firearms."

"This is for something else I have to do," she replied grimly.

"At Boweshoro?" He grinned at her. "Something to do with being an abolitionist maybe?"

She gave him a sharp look. "And if it is?"

"Look," he said, dropping the grin. "Where I come from we don't see any colored people and don't think about them much either. Oh, I know they're human beings, but they're still strangers to me. Sometimes I hear it said that the blacks can't think and understand things as well as whites do, or even feel as terribly as we would if we were in chains. I see you're shaking your head as if I should know better than to believe that." His grin came back, and he added, "Well, since I don't know better yet, and I'd like to, why don't you tell me about them now? There's a long march ahead of us and plenty of time to talk."

And indeed, there was a good deal of time to talk, much more than enough. Meanwhile, the road began to climb steadily. Higher and higher it wound between the mountain peaks on either side until it leveled out at last in a high valley. Just before sunset, men and horses shuffled wearily into the little town of Bowesboro. Its one and only street was empty. The barber shop, the general store, the little hotel—all were closed. Someone had torn Old Glory from the pole jutting out from the post office and hung the Confederate flag in its place. As an officer stood up on his horse to pull it down, two jeering children appeared from the alley behind it and began to sing "Dixie."

A glaring soldier raised his fist. "Maybe what you need is a real hiding!"

The boys set themselves to run. But meanwhile they sang louder.

> Old times there are not forgotten
> Look away, look away, look away Dixie land!"

When the soldier broke ranks to pounce on them, his sergeant shoved him back. "That ain't what you do!" he said.

An American flag lay crumpled and dirty on the ground where it had been thrown. The sergeant picked it up, kissed it tenderly, folded it, and tucked it in his shirt. Then he began to sing.

Oh, we'll rally round the flag, boys
We'll rally once again
Shouting the battle cry of Freeeeedom.

Everywhere up and down the line, men picked up their marching step and joined in.

The Union forever!
Hurray, boys! Hurrah!
Down with the traitors
And up with the Stars
Oh, we'll rally round the flag
Yes, we'll rally once again
Shouting the battle cry of Freeeeedom.

They marched out the other end of town still singing, but Hanna was not with them. Across the valley on a small knoll stood a white mansion, and spread out behind it were the low gray shacks of the slaves' quarters. She took the narrow road leading to it. But before she'd gone a quarter of a mile, the captain came galloping after her, with the carbine held high. "The major and I want you to have it back," he told her. "And he says that if you can break your friend loose and catch up to us, we'll see to it he gets down to the colored regiment Colonel Terwilliger is training. Good luck!"

SEVEN

Despite the advice from her grand-uncle, Hanna could not bring herself to do anything but head straight down the road toward the mansion.

Everything Rafe had told her about the five years he'd been a slave to Squire Bowes filled her with fury. He'd been kicked and beaten and half-starved. Worst of all, that cruel man had made a little boy believe the lie that his mammy was dead. Rafe couldn't have known how Rosalie, with Mama's help, was searching for him everywhere as they went about freeing other slaves. When Rosalie finally learned who his owner was, the Squire had agreed to sell her child back to her. But what did he do instead? He took the money she'd sent on ahead, then laid a trap to catch and hang her! *That* was when he told Rafe that his mama was really alive.

Why had Rafe been dragged back so many years after Rosalie had outwitted the Squire and freed her child? Why had the Squire paid a big reward to get him back? It had to be for revenge. So what was he going to do to Rafe—if he hadn't done it already? Blind him? Torture him? Hang Rafe from his highest tree as a warning to the other poor souls on his plantation not to even dream of escape? Maybe all of it! Hanna gripped the carbine. The more she thought of the Squire, the more she realized the power she had to simply wipe him and his overseers off the face of the earth.

A kind of madness was rising in her. It bubbled up from the power and fury boiling within her mind—and from the absolute rightness she saw in her cause.

It was the sudden appearance of the Conjure Woman that delivered her. In the dimming light, that ancient, wrinkled face floated for the briefest moment before Hanna's eyes, then flickered and was gone.

Was it only her imagination, or had the old lady passed on at last and this was her ghost? Hanna could not be sure of anything—except for the clear thought that she had other powers besides hatred and the ability to kill.

Turning into the trees, Hanna circled the edges of the great fields and gazed across them at the long rim of slave huts. Something seemed strange about them. Dead silence hung in the air. Night had barely fallen, yet no one moved, and no sounds seemed to come from within.

As she rode slowly along, the fields themselves drew her attention. How weedy and untended they looked! A huge barn loomed ahead. Hanna recalled being told it had been used for drying great leaves of tobacco to make cigars. Leaving Johnny Appleseed behind a bush, she opened the big door and looked inside. The long racks were still there, but nothing hung from them. What was going on?

A low whistle brought her horse. "I'm leaving you here for a while," she told him, gathering a few edible-looking plants and bringing them inside. "I'll need you to be quiet and very good," she said, kissing him. She stared at the carbine poking out of her saddlebag, wondering if she could trust herself with it. Grabbing it, she ran outside.

A quarter of a mile away, the slave huts stood out in the open, not at all close to the woods. Set back against the trees, where the slaves could be watched, were the cabins for the white overseers. Next to those cabins were the dog kennels. Hanna had no choice but to go past them.

Her best bet, she decided, was to crawl on her belly across the field, pushing the carbine in front of her and hoping she wouldn't have to fire at anybody. The going proved to be hard and tiring, but she kept at it. Thankfully, so far there were no dogs howling at the approach of a stranger. Suddenly there was a blur of something coming straight at her! She sprang to her knees, took aim—and heard a thin whine.

It was only an old mutt with a hanging belly and a hopeful look, wheezing up to her for a kind pat and a gentle word. Hanna gave him both, then decided to stand up and look around. What was going on in this place?

It was still too early in the evening for everyone to be sleeping, yet no lamps shone in the windows of the overseers' cabins. Nothing stirred in the kennels either. Were they all empty? Hanna ran the rest of the way to the rim of huts and ducked into each of them, one after the other. There was not a slave anywhere.

She turned her attention to the great manor house on the knoll. A light in a single window shone through the branches of a shade tree; otherwise everything there was dark too. With the mutt still trailing along behind her, Hanna headed for the tree. Setting the carbine against the trunk, she climbed up on a branch.

She saw a man at a table, playing cards with someone she could not see. This must have been the Squire, for there was the pointy white beard and messy white hair she had heard about. Just the sight of him made her angry.

Squire Bowes wore a white linen suit that must have been very expensive but was now scruffy and dirty. His little round eyes stared over the stub of a dead cigar at the cards he was being dealt. He looked at them, chewed his cigar, threw two of them down, and picked up two more. As he put them into their right places, a smile began to curl up from the corners of his mouth and he said something. Then his smile froze into a look of disgust.

While the Squire reached for a flask of brandy, the man Hanna hadn't been able to see before leaned across the table to gather in the chips he had just won. First came his dark-skinned arms, bound together at the wrists by a thick iron chain. Then came his head and face. Hanna gasped. The other poker player was Rafe Sims!

Hanna wasted no time climbing down, scooping up her carbine, and dashing for the door of the manor house. The huge rooms she passed through were completely empty. Not a stick of furniture remained.

Ahead there were voices, Rafe saying, "You lose five more hands, and I go free."

"Not if I find you're cheatin' on me."

"If anyone is cheating, it isn't me."

"Do I hear you correctly? Are you calling your own master a card cheat? Why, if I was, you'd have lost every hand!"

"Oh, I don't think you're stacking the cards to *win*."

"What are you saying? That I *want* to let you go?"

"I think you do. I think you know it's the right thing to do."

"Thunderation, no! I don't think it's the right thing. I just don't know as I care to give you to that bunch of swine who cheated me at poker and took everything I have."

"Then why did you pay the reward to have me brought back?" Rafe asked.

"I didn't pay the reward. I *owe* the reward. Let *them* pay it. And I did it because they knew about you. You are what they call a financial asset. I have to turn over all of my assets to cover my losses! I figure you are such a bad nigger, just like your mother, that you'll make them rue the day I ever sent *this* asset to them! Now why don't you just shut up and deal?"

"I think he'd deal better," declared Hanna, aiming the carbine as she walked in, "if you'd unlock his chains."

Rafe pushed himself to his feet, crying, "Hanna-Anna!"

"Even now, you can't stop calling me that?" she said with a grin.

Squire Bowes wasn't too unhappy about letting his recaptured slave go. It would serve them right, those people who'd be coming in the morning to take everything else he owned, said the Squire, "even the gold fillings from my teeth! But I need you to tie me up so nobody can say I did it myself."

The two friends were glad to oblige. They used the shackles that had bound Rafe hand and foot. But when

Hanna emptied his pockets, the Squire began to whine. "That twenty dollars is all I have left in the world."

"Consider it a down payment on what you stole from Rafe's mother when she tried to buy his freedom!" Hanna snapped.

Leaving him there, they brought Johnny Appleseed out of the tobacco barn and headed off after the major's marching column. Taking turns riding the strong but elderly horse, they moved slowly through the night, talking quietly, sharing the stories of their lives since they were last together.

They went on like this for as long as they could hold out. But the mostly level valley had narrowed. New peaks were closing in on both sides, and the road began to rise and curve. Higher and higher they went. Just as they were reaching a level place at the top, Johnny Appleseed, who seemed to be walking in his sleep, stumbled over a deep rut in the road and nearly fell.

"He'll grow lame if we don't stop," Hanna said.

Weary themselves, they led him through the bushes to a small clearing and took off his saddle. Hanna settled down with her head against one side of the saddle while Rafe took the other. "Good night," they told each other, closing their eyes and clasping each other's hands.

"What's *that?*" Hanna said suddenly, aware of a curious rumbling in the ground. Rafe felt it too, and he sat up. But Johnny Appleseed was ahead of them both. His ears had perked up at sounds they did not hear. He gave a soft whinny and fell silent.

"Horses," whispered Rafe.

"But where?"

The snapping of dry brushwood answered her question. They were climbing up the other side of the hill. Hanna jumped up quickly and put her hand on Johnny Appleseed's white diamond. He lowered himself to his knees. Moments later, the rising shapes of many horses and men appeared close by on the road.

"Well, gentlemen," the two friends heard, "as we can finally tell from this height, there are no Yankee battalions following the one that went down to the railroad. That leaves us free to attack without worrying about our backs. Although we are still outnumbered, we have two main advantages. They do not have the high ground and they do not know we are here. We must gallop down into their encampment while they are sleeping, and it must be a total surprise."

"Surely they have posted sentrics, Colonel. If they give the alarm too soon "

"I am well aware of that. Make sure to get the corporal who used to be a tracker. The one the men call Moccasin."

Rafe seized Hanna tightly by the arm. And as soon as she heard the voice of the man who'd been sent for, she recognized him too. This was the same bounty hunter who had shot Rosalie!

"I reckon I know what y'all got in mind, Colonel," he said. "My two nephews an' me, we done got 'em spotted already. They out thar in the starlight jest as long in the neck as turkeys."

"I'm afraid we can't have a turkey shoot, Corporal. And no screams either."

"'Why, that ain't no kind of problem a-tall. A man with his throat slit open don't sing 'John Brown's Body' when he falls."

"Very good. Our men will spread out and follow you down within a hundred yards. Your signal that all is clear will be what?"

The ex-tracker chuckled. "Well, Colonel, maybe I could toss a scalp."

"Just send one of your nephews. Yes, Major, what is it?"

"Surely we are too far behind the lines to take prisoners and send them back."

"Yes, we are, and that is not our purpose. Those Yankee troops down there have not yet been hardened in battle. If we kill a great many of them in a very short time, the rest will scatter in terror. So far we have only been attacking supply wagons, derailing trains, cutting telegraph wires, and the like. But we need a military victory here on Kentucky soil, gentlemen. It doesn't matter that it will be a small one. Corporal, you and I and your nephews are the only ones in this force who are natives of Kentucky. Explain to these gentlemen of the deep South what will happen if we rout those Yankees tonight."

"Thousands of right-thinkin' white folks will be comin' down out of the hills 'gainst the federal gov'ment, that's what. An uprisin' fer sure."

"Exactly. Thank you, Corporal. You may get started, and we will follow."

The colonel waited until Moccasin had departed. "An uprising, gentlemen," he repeated. "Let us go now and bear in mind what we can accomplish this night!"

The instant they were gone, Hanna threw the saddle over her horse, saying, "Help me with the straps."

Rafe grabbed her by the arm. "Now listen!" he hissed. "This is what I came down from Canada for—to fight! Give me that repeating gun. I'll take the horse and you stay here."

"We're going to warn them together. Don't argue with me!"

"Hanna, are you willing to die tonight?"

"If I have to."

"But I don't *want* that. Can't you understand? I don't want it!" His eyes glistened. He was forcing back tears. "There's going to be a lot of killing. And I couldn't stand it if—"

"You don't have to frighten me any more than I already am. I'm scared for you too."

"If you die," he almost sobbed, "I'll kill you."

"Same here." She pressed his arm, murmuring, "If I never see you after this . . ."

"I know."

Hanna bit her lip before she said, "Listen, if we see they're going to stop us, we have to make them shoot. We can't let them stop us quietly."

"Okay. But before they get me, I want to fight!"

"All right, take the carbine. I've got the horse pistol. Let's mount up."

The raiders were avoiding the open road that led to the encampment, and for good reason. From the moment Hanna and Rafe rode onto it they were in terrible danger of being spotted from the woods. For a long while their breathless good fortune seemed to hold. The deserted pike sloped downward into a short, level stretch, then bent around and dipped again.

Yet there was no way to disguise the sound of a cantering horse. It was not a nearby rifle that sent a bullet of hot terror into the pit of Hanna's stomach, but the snapping of a man's fingers. Clearly, unspoken orders were being given. At the end of the next long turn in the road, three horsemen crossed from the left and swept in front of them.

"Give up now and we won't hurt you," a voice from behind them called softly. They were about to be surrounded.

"Never!" cried Rafe, wielding the carbine. But before he could shoot, the butt end of a thrown pistol crashed into the center of his back. The gun clattered to the ground. As he fell forward against Hanna, she swung left on the reins and dug her heels into Johnny Appleseed's sides. The bolting horse leaped through a thick tangle of thornbush that ripped flesh from his sides, then plunged on.

"Rafe, stop swaying or you'll fall off!"

"Forget about me and fire your damned horse pistol!"

"I don't even know if it works!" Freeing one hand, Hanna reached into the saddlebag, brought it out, aimed it through the tall pines at the sky—and did nothing.

"Why don't you shoot?"

"I get just one chance. Suppose these trees kill the sound of it?"

"Hanna, think about why we haven't been shot dead yet!"

She pulled the trigger. The loud report echoed away, then died. The grim chase continued in silence. But only until a bugle sounded below. The shot had been heard. The Union troops were being called to alert.

The raiders' commanding officer now had to choose between calling off the attack or ordering a wild and valiant charge down into the waiting encampment. Raising his sword, he pointed it ahead, shouting, "Victory or death!" A bloodcurdling yell rose up all around Hanna and Rafe. Amid the din of charging horses and men, a single rebel officer galloped up to them, the recovered carbine in his hand.

There was nowhere for them to go. No chance to escape. Two shots and it would all be over. Hanna's gaze met that of the young rebel. "My compliments," he said, taking his cap off. "Bravery must be admired, even among enemies." Then, waving her carbine in the air, he galloped off to kill or be killed.

Well, to be brave was one thing; to be foolish was another. What good would it do to hurl themselves down into the battle unarmed? Hanna and Rafe rushed through the trees to a rocky ledge hanging over the valley. Below, though they could barely see any of it in the twinkling starlight, lay the Union encampment.

There was no shooting yet, as frantic Union men tumbled out of tents, grabbing rifles from stacks. In their grogginess, they tumbled over one another. Many of them fumbled with bayonets while officers screamed not to waste time. With sergeants shoving them into place, they ran to form two lines, one behind the other, facing the hill. As the first line kneeled into firing position, the terrifying rebel yell went up again. But what, in all this darkness, were the Union men to aim at?

At the very moment the enemy came galloping up, a flare shot into the sky from a special pistol in the Union major's hand burst into light. Suddenly night turned into day over the charging raiders and the quarter mile of open ground between them and the Union men taking aim. The first line fired, then hurried to reload while the second line shot past them.

Up on the ridge, Hanna covered her eyes, though that could not shield her from the rising smell of gunpowder and the screams of death. Rafe sat with his arm around her, staring until the flare died out, leaving only the flashes of gunfire to see by. Below him, the galloping Confederate raiders who were still unhurt or able to fight on despite their wounds leaped over the bodies of fallen comrades and into the camp, some firing, some swinging sabers. Everything depended on whether the young Union foot soldiers would stand and fight or break and run.

Both firing lines were wavering. Men were on their feet, some too scared to fix bayonets. Then the major dashed out ahead of them. A sergeant followed, and the Union troops burst forward, screaming like devils to drown out the rebels' yell. The battle became a free-for-all, where rifles were only good for jabbing or knocking men off their mounts and pistols could be fired into faces that looked little different from one's own.

By now, Hanna had forced herself to watch whatever could be seen. One way or another, she was as much a part of this war as she had been part of the Underground Railroad in the days when it was thought that slavery could still come to a peaceful end. Below her, the fighting dragged on. Dawn came, revealing bodies strewn everywhere. From the Union camp came no shouts of victory, although there certainly had been one. Only a small band of Confederate horses and men could be seen straggling away from the dwindling line of fire. On the other side of the railroad tracks, the digging of graves had already begun.

Hanna wept as she watched. Rafe held her. "In the history books," she said, "this war always seems glorious."

"Are you sorry you came back?"

It took her a long while to answer with a shake of her head. "I found you. And I'm not going to stop till I find Papa and Mama."

Rafe had a sore back, but it was Johnny Appleseed who worried them. Though the bleeding from his cuts had stopped, he'd gone lame. Carrying the saddle to lighten his step, they led him slowly the rest of the way into the camp.

From where he stood before a command tent, the major waved them over. "I believe we have recovered your carbine," he said with a smile.

A hideous thought raced through her mind. But Hanna could not bring herself to ask whether any Union soldiers had been killed with her weapon.

"We took it from a lieutenant who said you were the one

who fired the shot that gave the alarm. It saved our hash, and I am most grateful to you. To both of you."

Rafe drew his first satisfied breath since being arrested while trying to enlist. But Hanna was anxious about the man who had let them live. "That lieutenant—I hope he's all right?"

"No, I'm afraid he died. They were extremely courageous men, and I take no joy in their misfortune. We suffered sad losses too, of course. But we have come out of this fight a stronger force."

He put out his hand to Rafe. "Welcome, Mr. Sims. I already know what you have suffered to take your rightful place among us. It makes me all the more ashamed that many in this country and this army do not yet understand the very freedom we are fighting for. Sadly, it is only because we have been losing this war that some members of your race are being allowed to take up arms and fight. They are being set apart in special units commanded by white officers, like Colonel Terwilliger. I believe he is leading his regiment somewhere east of Memphis. Hopefully, there will be a train here shortly. When it turns back south, you will come with us as far as that city and be sent on to his unit."

Hanna stiffened, and Rafe calmed her with a touch. "I suppose, Major, that you could issue a uniform and rifle to me now?"

"Given what you've already done, I suppose I could go against regulations. You might, however, find yourself in a fight of your own."

That smoky look came into Rafe's eyes. "I'll take my

chances." Hanna knew he would have liked to add, "So will anyone who starts it."

But no one did. Not when word spread through the ranks of what the "singing nurse" and the colored fellow with burning eyes had done to save their hash.

EIGHT

It took another full day and night before an iron horse came chugging up the track through a cloud of its own smoke. Strung out along both sides of the long train was a detachment of horsemen that had been guarding it from attack for hundreds of miles. But these soldiers of the United States' First Kentucky Cavalry did not have a pair of riding boots or a uniform among them.

The officer who rode up to salute the colonel had spurs strapped to his bare feet. He wore a big floppy hat and a shirt the reddish color of hickory wood. Tucked inside the top of a pair of britches that his own ma or sister had spun were two pistols. In one hand, he held the long Kentucky rifle his pioneer grandpa had long ago used to fight off Indians while driving his family westward in a covered wagon.

The wood-burning engine pulled dozens of empty passenger cars. While the troops were getting ready to board, Hanna helped a wounded soldier limp to a car where the seats had been pulled out and cots set in their place. Meanwhile, no one except Rafe paid much attention to the fifty or so black people who had ridden the train in open flat cars, sitting on top of piles of metal.

"We're turnin' around; this is as far as you go," Rafe heard the conductor tell them, waving for everyone to get off.

One of them raised a confused voice. "But kin you tell us, suh, where we goes now?"

"That's entirely up to you. You wanted to be taken north. This is as far north as we go. Our part of the bargain is kept."

Rafe stepped in front of him. "What bargain was that?"

The conductor looked him up and down before answering. "These contrabands—" he began.

"You mean runaways?"

"That's right. There's a whole lot of them who want to get out of Tennessee in case the rebels win it back from General Sherman. None of them had any money, but the engineer said to pick the fifty strongest to hammer down new sections of track anywhere raiders tore the old ones up ahead of us." The conductor started to walk away, saying, "They've got nothing to complain about. They've all been fed pretty good and not one of them was hit by the gunfire."

All that morning Johnny Appleseed had been walking along docilely behind Hanna. But a particularly shiny button on Rafe's military jacket caught his eye, and he shoved his head between the two of them. He was still trying to nibble on it when they walked up to the freight car where the officers' horses were being loaded on.

"Better lead that stallion up the ramp yourself," the colonel told her. "He looks skittish to me."

Johnny Appleseed had gone pop-eyed at the sight of those wooden boards. Even with Hanna holding the bridle and coaxing him, it was one step up, two steps back. "Come on, now, this is nothing like that nasty old ferry," she told him.

"Just think about apples and maple sugar treats." But nothing worked, until she whispered furiously into his ear, "Don't you *dare* embarrass me!"

She needn't have worried about the colonel laughing at her. He was too busy listening to Rafe's account of the homeless and penniless "contrabands" who were being dumped in these hills with nowhere to go and nothing to get there with.

"That's true, this isn't much of a beginning for a life of freedom," the colonel admitted with a sigh. "But all I can do for them, I'm afraid, is leave a portion of our food and blankets behind."

"With all respect, sir, that isn't enough. Look at my own case. I've had some education. I know how to get around and do things. Yet I was captured and beaten and shipped back into slavery—and that was up in Indiana! Kentucky is practically at war with itself. These people are in danger for their lives. They need weapons to protect themselves."

"Don't you know better, private, than to suggest an officer should give away his army's hardware?" The colonel's stern expression only lasted long enough for a sly grin to pass between himself and the young captain who'd returned Hanna's carbine. "On the other hand, the *rebel* guns that have been collected are another matter. The captain here will go with you to round them up. But do it quickly. We'll be leaving within the hour."

"Thank you, sir!"

"Private Sims!" said Hanna, before he could go off. "I am surprised you are forgetting Squire Bowes's contribution to

115

the cause." A little tug brought the purse up from under her collar, and she poured into his hand the twenty dollars that had been in the slaveowner's pockets when she'd turned them inside out.

"Oh, I think we can do a bit better than that," declared the captain as he set out with Rafe to round up the captured weapons. By the time the food, blankets, and guns were handed out, the men had chipped in almost two hundred dollars more.

Rafe told Hanna all about it later on, when he joined her in the caboose, where she was sitting with the wounded. One of them had been teaching himself to read from a book called *The Adventures of Robinson Crusoe*. She'd been helping him sound out the words, but now three others wanted her to read it aloud. This she did until her eyes grew tired because of the jogging of the train. When Rafe took over, the men stared at him, surprised that a black person could read.

The hours went by slowly. Peacefully too, if nobody counted the sniper fire that broke a window now and then and sent the soldiers diving from their hardwood seats. There was only one stop, to lay new tracks. When Rafe got out to join the volunteers, Hanna went through the rattling train to the officers' car. From there she brought back ink bottles, writing quills, and a thick stack of paper. While the men wrote letters home, Hanna quietly began to draw them. When Rafe returned later, she sketched him too.

"Could you draw a picture of *yourself*, Miss Hanna?" the owner of the book asked.

"Yes, one for each of us," pleaded another man.

A private who served as a medic rustled up his shaving mirror, and Hanna worked at her sketches far into the dwindling daylight, as Rafe watched. When the last and best of her sketches was done, she quietly handed it to him. He tucked it away in his chest pocket, then went back through the passenger cars looking for a place to sit.

Hanna pushed the empty wooden crate she'd been sitting on against a wall, rolled a blanket into a pillow, and leaned against it. But it was hard to fall asleep. When one of the wounded began to moan in pain, she sat up completely.

A medic was bending over the man. "Leg acting up, soldier?"

"What are you talking about? I got bone sticking straight through my skin, and the painkiller's wore off! Can you give me some more?"

"All gone. I'm sorry. Those two bottles we had went missing, and I don't know where."

"Oh, dear God!"

"You've got to hold on. Soon as we get down to Memphis, a doc's gonna set it to heal up just fine."

"Tell me *another* fairy tale, why don't you? Those sawbones will want to hack it off. And I don't want that! I just don't want it!"

"Fer argument's sake now, let's say it's so. Why, that might be the luckiest thang ever happened to a feller in your situation. The *Red Rover* will whisk you straight upriver to one of them recuperatin' hospitals, and the war will be all over fer you."

"So will everything else! Do you think I'm going to let them take my leg when I'm engaged to be married!"

"If I was your sweetheart," said Hanna, going up to him, "all I'd really care about was having you back."

"You think so?"

She took his hand. "Yes, I do, and I'd love you just as much. Now let's speak more softly so the others can sleep. Why don't you tell me about her?"

Hanna stayed with the man until he passed out again. Then she dozed for a bit until he awoke once more in pain. By that time, up and down the many passenger cars, the men were being roused. Through a shot-out window came the not very distant toot of a Mississippi riverboat. They were pulling into Memphis.

It was like pulling into a sprawling city of army tents set up outside the town. A single word exploded in Hanna's mind and almost burst from her lips: "Mama!"

Anxiously, she looked for the part of the camp that had been set aside for patients, ambulances, doctors, and nurses. The medics on board needed to know the same thing. When the train stopped, the hospital area was pointed out to them by an officer who came forward to salute the colonel. As soon as the wounded were carried or helped off, or got off by themselves using rifles for crutches, they headed for it.

Hanna walked beside the stretcher bearing the man with the broken leg, promising to send a letter to his sweetheart. Meanwhile she glanced anxiously into every tent. A nurse in long black robes came out of one and asked if she was looking for someone.

"Yes! Dora Terwilliger."

"I don't know that name, I'm sorry. Is she one of us?"

"Well, she was leading some wagons that were bringing down supplies."

"What organization would that be? We are from the Sisters of Charity. Might she be from the Christian Association?"

"No . . . uh . . . the Sanitary Commission."

Another black-robed woman came to the front of the tent. "I think I may have heard the name Terwilliger," she said. Her hand went to her chin. "No, no. On second thought, that was an officer. I'm sorry."

"Wait, please! Could that be Colonel Amos Terwilliger?"

"I don't think I ever heard his first name, but he *was* a colonel."

"Where did you see him?"

"At the Battle of Shiloh in April. A very unusual man, the way he looked after his own wounded. That regiment is here right now—well, what remains of it. But I believe he left his command to form a new regiment elsewhere." Her gaze dropped and she fell silent.

"Of black troops?"

"Yes."

"That's him! That's my father!" The pride with which she proclaimed it made both nurses smile. "Do you know where they are now?"

"No. But I'm sure you can find out from the camp's commanding officer. And if you want to know about Dora Terwilliger, go into the chief surgeon's tent and get his staff

119

sergeant to check the roster. You may have to bribe him with something. If you wait a moment, I think I have a bag of rock candies that will tempt him."

"He will do anything for a sweet," agreed the other nurse. "As you will see from the condition of his teeth."

As it turned out, the rock candies were wasted on the staff sergeant's wobbling molars. Yes, he knew head nurse Terwilliger by sight, he said. But neither she nor any of her nurses and wagons had shown up yet. "Never can tell what will get through and what won't," he added. "Medical supplies is worth more 'n gold in some places. They's lots of it what goes south after some enterprisin' land or river pirate sets his mind to get his hands on it."

Keeping busy was the only answer for Hanna's worries, and she lost no time trying to find out where to look for her father. Papa was much easier to locate, give or take twenty miles or so. Although the war had gone into a kind of lull since the Battle of Shiloh, he and his recruits had been in a series of "small" battles at a place called Satan's Hollow in high country to the east. "Only a few regiments are in it on either side," the commanding officer's adjutant had told her. "Doesn't much matter whether we win or lose there. But it gives us a chance to see how well these Negroes will fight."

Hanna didn't like the sneering way he'd said the word "Negroes" or the contempt he showed for a white officer who was willing to serve in battle with black troops.

"I'm going to make a guess in three parts," she told him. "The first part is that you were never in any battle at all.

120

The second is that just the *thought* of being in one makes your stomach flop over. The third is that if you ever *had* been in a battle, you'd never be able to say that it didn't matter whether you won it or lost it." She didn't have to wait for him to tell her if she was right or wrong. It was enough to see his lips quiver before she turned and stiffly walked out.

The camp was so vast that it took a long time to find the battalion she had arrived with. They were already set up in tents. Hanna saw Rafe coming out of the colonel's tent with an envelope in his hand. "This is for me to show your father. Now all I have to do is find him."

"Well, I know where to go looking," she said. "But we need Johnny Appleseed. I haven't seen him anywhere. Didn't anyone take him off the train?"

An answering whinny came from behind a nearby tent. "Calm down, boy," said a familiar voice as the captain led him over. "Find your mama, Hanna?"

"No, and I'm worried about her. But if I just stay around here waiting, I'll go crazy. I'm going with Rafe to see Papa."

"Is he in action?"

"Yes."

"Then always make sure to duck the cannon balls and jump over the minnie balls."

"What are minnie balls?"

"Oh, you'll know them when they come bowling down at you."

"Sure hope so. Give me your cheek."

"Is this going to be a kiss?"

"No, a wipe," she said, dabbing at his face with a thumb. "You've a smudge."

"You've got more than one yourself. Have you thought of changing out of those duds?"

"Oh, Lord!" Hanna exploded, glancing down at herself for the first time in who knew how long.

"I shouldn't have mentioned it," the captain said with a gallant smile. "You still look like the fairest flower of the midwest."

But her frown didn't melt. "Some flower! Look at me! I'll have to go clear across this camp again to beg the Sisters of Charity for some women's clothes. Say, you wouldn't have something I could wear, would you?"

"Me?"

"Well, if you could spare it. I'm fairly tall for a girl, and . . ."

"Hey, you don't have to pretend I'm not short. It's what saved my life back in that fight. A bullet knocked my cap off. See?" he said, holding out his hat. "It went in this side, came out the other, and left my hair with a part. Come inside my tent."

"No, *I'll* go in. You just tell me where to look."

When Hanna came out again, she was dressed in a soldier's uniform. "All I need now is a hat with two bullet holes for ventilation," she declared. The captain grinned as he handed it over.

Next Hanna went with Rafe to take their leave of the colonel. He came out of his tent looking very concerned. "I'm told there isn't a road behind our lines where the rebels don't come out during the daytime and *stay* out all night.

You really ought to wait for a patrol going in that direction."

An officer who was visiting from another regiment shook his head. "I wouldn't say that's any safer, Colonel. There's nothing those rebs like better to fall upon than our patrols."

"In that case . . . why does she keep leaving behind what every well-bred young lady needs nowadays?" Ducking back into his tent, the colonel brought out her carbine. "It's fully loaded, I checked. Let's hope you don't have to use it." He turned to Rafe. "What a blood-boiling sight *you'll* make on the road, Private Sims. A colored man in uniform—and traveling with a white woman!"

"That's one of the reasons I've put on a uniform," declared Hanna.

"Oh, sure, that will make a very great difference—people will be trying to shoot the two of you down from their front porches."

Hanna and Rafe exchanged glances, and that smoky look came into his eyes. "Maybe it's better I go alone," Rafe told her. "*Nobody's* making me take this uniform off now that I got it."

"We'll stay off the roads," Hanna said.

The colonel sighed and gave up. "I believe I understand your feelings, Private Sims. You earned that uniform. Do us proud in it."

"Be proud to," Rafe said, saluting. The colonel returned the salute, and Rafe and Hanna led Johnny Appleseed away, saying other good-byes as they went.

At the edge of the camp, Hanna was turning to put her foot into the stirrup when Rafe stopped her cold. "If we're going to ride together, Hanna, I'll ride in front and *you* can hold on."

"All right. You don't have to bite my head off. What's wrong with you?"

"Ain't nothin' wrong with me," Rafe said, swinging into the saddle and stretching out his arm. "You goin' take my hand or not?"

"I'm taking it. I'm taking it."

He gave her a tug, and she plunked down behind him. "Giddyap, horse!" He dug his heels hard into Johnny Appleseed, who took off like a shot across an open field.

"Rafe, we've got a long distance to go on him. You can't push him like that."

"Be quiet."

In heavy silence, they rode through long rows of cornstalks, broke through a border of tall pines, and dashed in and out of the shade of a weeping willow.

"Rafe, have I hurt your feelings in some way?" Hanna asked.

"What, by swinging your hips into somebody's tent and putting on his clothes and rolling your eyes and saying, 'Give me your cheek, sir' like you was going to plant a big kiss?"

She gritted her teeth. "Rafe, I didn't roll my eyes, and—"

"Don't tell me. I saw it."

"—and I didn't plant any kiss."

"No, but you were laying it on him pretty good!"

"Rafe, are you *jealous?*"

"Jealous? Who, me? No! You want to go vamping

124

somebody, that's your business. You go right ahead."

"Vamping? What's vamping?"

"I have said all I'm goin' to say."

"If you mean *flirting*, Rafe, I don't think I was doing that. But I have a right to, you know. I'm coming into the age where girls do begin to flirt. And—" Her finger shot past his head. "Watch out for that ditch."

"I'm watching. I'm watching."

"And slow down too, please. But gently. Don't pull so hard on his mouth."

"Yas'm, Missy Hanna."

"Cut that out! I just happen to know my horse a little better than you do."

"Then maybe you know all this yelling is scaring him. Slow down, Johnny Appleseed." Rafe stroked the horse's withers. "We're not really mad at each other. Things are the way they are, that's all."

Hanna tightened her hold around his waist and laid her face against Rafe's shoulder. "Tell me what I'm supposed to do about you when I know your great-great-great-something grandson. I already know some of your history. You stay on in this century and you get married and grow old . . . and the whole thing."

"Oh, and I suppose you're gonna take that captain back with you when you skip ahead again?"

"Oh, Rafe," she cried, "maybe I should just stay here. Maybe this is where I belong. Just like you do."

"Hey, don't go by what I had to do. Punching kids out in the schoolyard and bopping to the movies wasn't taking my mind off seeing those slave trackers shoot down my mother. But when you landed in the future you didn't remember a thing about who you were. You were the luckiest person in the world that the Posts found you and took you into their family. So tell me how you can just walk away from them forever?"

"What is it with you? Doesn't it matter to you that I'm here?"

"Sure it does, Hanna-Anna, but—"

"That's not my name!"

"But it's what you are, half one, half the other. You're at *least* half Anna Post for sure."

"Well, that's not how I feel right now!" she shouted.

She would have burst into tears if she hadn't noticed that they were being watched from the next line of trees.

"Look," she said, pointing past him at the amazed black faces of two children. The children darted away from them, disappearing below a dip in the land. Riding toward it themselves, Rafe and Hanna heard what sounded like the crack of a door and then uneasy voices.

Then they saw a row of shacks. Folks of all ages came out of them and immediately fell silent.

"Slaves," Rafe said, and broke into a sigh. "Why do they stay here with our army so close that they could get away?"

"Maybe their masters ran off."

"Could be."

As the pair drew alongside the cabins, Rafe raised his musket to them in a salute. Heads turned slowly as they went by. But other than that, no one moved.

126

It was a very little girl perched in her daddy's big clasped hands like a bird in a nest who changed all that. She waved her tiny fingers at them. When Hanna waved back, many arms went up in the air.

A youth of Hanna's age called out to Rafe, "You a honest-to-God Yankee soldier, brother?"

"Sure am, brother."

They moved on. Behind them, a woman began to sing:

> *When Israel was in Egypt land*
> *Let my people go*
> *Oppressed so hard they could not stand*
> *Let my people go*
> *Go down, Moses!*
> *Way down in Egypt Land*
> *And tell ol' Pharaoh*
> *To let my people go!*

Rafe had been a little child the last time he'd cried in Hanna's arms. Holding him now from behind, she felt his chest quiver and she wondered whether there were tears in his eyes. But she knew he'd never show her if there were.

The long ride over rolling land went on hour after hour. The pair kept away from the open road as much as they could. But the ground grew rockier and more tiring for Johnny Appleseed. Thickening clouds made it harder to tell directions by the sun. Hanna pulled out a rough map that the commander's adjutant had drawn for her. Before it grew too dark to find, Rafe guided the horse onto the road to Satan's Hollow.

Dusk was probably the most dangerous time to be out. They held their guns ready and each studied a different side of the road. But luck seemed to be with them. The oncoming night was so black that it was soon impossible to see the difference between road and tree and sky.

"If it's too dark for us to keep going, it's the same for anybody else," murmured Rafe as they dismounted to feel around for a tree against which to rest until dawn.

But as it turned out, others had reckoned differently. Others had known how, on a Tennessee night in late summer, the clouds could thin out enough for the stars to dance. They also knew there would be a full moon. Yet how did those Confederates steal up on the sleeping pair so silently? Hanna was aware of nothing until the end of a rifle barrel prodded her in the face.

"Git up, nigger, and git yerself hung!" said a second man, who was standing over Rafe.

"I'm a *soldier*," Rafe hissed at him. "Shoot me like one."

"You ain't never gonna be no soldier. Don't care what you got on. Now I said—"

It was then that Hanna's mind lost contact with the order in which things were happening. For years to come she would try to sort it out. The stone that suddenly came flying like an arrow out of nowhere—had she seen it *before* it smashed into the head of the man standing over Rafe? And Rafe's screaming, "Duck, Hanna!"—was that while he was hurling himself upon the one who was about to shoot her, or were they already fighting? And when the fired rifle blew bark off the tree where her head had just been—was it just about then that the black stranger got up from the bushes with a slingshot in his hand? Or was that while she was rolling away to grab the carbine? She would never be able to put together the way it all happened before she fired off those bullets and kept blasting away until everything became very, very still.

NINE

The man who'd been knocked down by the flying rock had begun to stir. But it wasn't because of him that Hanna's heart had stopped. The other rebel lay on his face, perfectly still, with blood trickling through his hair. Was he dead?

After taking away their guns, Rafe bent over him and said, "It's only a cut. He's pretending."

"Well, ye cain't blame a feller fer tryin', kin ye? I sure am thankful fer her not bein' much of a shot with that dang repeater."

"That's how I *meant* to shoot," she snapped. "Raise your hands!"

Handing the guns to Hanna, Rafe tied the rebels' wrists behind their backs with the rope they would have used to hang him. Once he'd jerked them to their feet, he waited until Hanna mounted up, then fastened the other end of the rope to the pommel of Johnny Appleseed's saddle. The stranger, meanwhile, had fetched the rebels' horses. He and Rafe mounted up, and they all set out under a star-bright sky.

Till now, not a word had passed between the two friends and the owl-eyed man who had saved their lives. He only nodded when they thanked him. When at last he did speak, it was with a terrible stammer. Slowly they learned that his name was Aaron Johnston. He was a runaway from a cotton plantation down in Alabama. He'd come this far to join one of the colored Union regiments that all the slaves were whispering about. To get this far he'd been walking by night, hiding by day—and using his slingshot to bring down a rabbit or wild turkey whenever it was safe to build a cooking fire. If he could have one wish granted before he died, it was to be a free man fighting against slavery.

The road climbed steadily toward the high country. It was not too long afterward that they began to hear the distant crackle of rifle fire. Rafe, who had done some reading about this war, didn't think it was a full-sized battle. It was more likely that both sides were sending out small patrols at night to test each other's whereabouts. They'd exchange a few shots, then fall back to their own lines and report.

"The real fighting will come in the morning."

Aaron Johnston's fist curled tightly around his newfound rifle. "I . . . sh-sh-sho will be ready," he said. "You j-j-just t-t-teach me how to shoot."

They were still climbing when, in the darkness just before dawn, a silence fell among the hilltops that could have been the stillness of death. No bugle sounded reveille, yet everywhere they saw uniformed black men rise silently from their tents, seize their weapons, and slip like shadows into a deep thicket. By the hundreds they moved among the swirling mists, none of them speaking. It was as if not one of them dared to breathe.

Somewhere an order was being given, and Hanna heard the low metal clash of bayonets being fixed. She thought she glimpsed an officer's white glove being raised to lead the way into depths she could not see. The men were moving out. They disappeared into a blackness where no starlight shone. Where were these troops going? Was her Papa leading them? Had that been *his* raised arm?

Meanwhile the three friends, with the prisoners ahead of them, climbed higher toward the ridge ahead. The woods were thinner here, and the grassy places were turning rocky. As the first light of dawn crept out of the highlands in front of them, the sky itself suddenly seemed to crack open with an incredible roar. It was the voice of many enemy cannons letting loose at once. They spoke with one long, rolling voice—the voice of war.

"Get down!" Rafe screamed at her before she heard the whistling sound of an oncoming shell. But it was too late. There was a deafening explosion—and then nothing.

She awakened in an officer's arms. There was blood gushing from his own face but he was running with her. He was bearded and old enough, but he was not Papa!

"Rafe?" she tried to scream out above the din of the bombardment. Immediately her head began to feel as if it would explode.

"You're alive. Good." The officer's voice had an echo. "Who's Rafe . . . Rafe . . . Rafe . . . Ra . . . ?"

Hanna's voice came in gasps. "Private Sims, the soldier who was with me. And there was another man . . . and two prisoners."

His echoing words came in a jumble. Was he saying that he hadn't seen any of them? That he supposed they all got it?

"What are you talking about?" she shrieked in spite of the

pain. "He lives on and has children. He has grandchildren!"

"You know, I'll bet you're right. I'll go back and look for him, I promise. Just as soon as I get you to the White House."

White House? What was that? Was he taking her to the President? But White House was the name soldiers gave to any medical station near a battlefield. As he carried her into this one, an orderly pointed toward several stretchers lying on the open ground inside the circle of tents.

"Who are you looking for?" the officer asked when she raised herself on her elbows as soon as he'd set her down.

"My horse. I must have fallen off Johnny Appleseed. Didn't he follow me?"

"Well, maybe so. Tell you what. I'll go back and look for Johnny Appleseed too." He stared at her closely. "My God, you're just a child! What are you looking for now?"

"Colonel Amos Terwilliger. He's my father."

"I can't get your father for you now," he said softly. "There's going to be an assault on the enemy's positions and he's with his men, leading it. I am Major Clayton, adjutant to the general. I'll look in on you later. Or when you're better you may come to see me at the command tent. Meanwhile, I want you to lie still until the doctor can look at you. I have a daughter about your age, and if ever she came to find me here, I would fall apart were she to be injured. Bless you, child." He kissed her brow before he left, and Hanna sank into deep, dark sleep.

How many hours passed before the pelting of rain in her face woke her up, Hanna could not know. But lying all around her were wounded men who had not been there before. Their moans and shrieks of pain could be heard everywhere. Men cried out in the voices of small children for their mothers. Others wept for their wives. Hanna scrambled to her feet in spite of her lingering headache and went to them. She stroked many a cold, damp brow, and wiped the rain from their eyes, and spoke to them, soothing their hearts. But the screams that came from the operating tents, where so many arms and legs were being sawed off, tore at her own heart.

The worst of it was that she alone knew how needless almost all of these amputations were. If this were a hundred fifty years from now, there would be antibiotics to fight infections before they could spread, and even schoolchildren would know something about keeping germs away from injuries! Wherever Hanna glanced in the operating tents she saw a doctor (there were only two of them) running from one patient to another without washing his hands. His saws, pliers, and even his hands were filthy with the last man's ooze. He used unwashed bandages and sponges that had been taken from someone else.

Finally Hanna could be silent no longer. Just as the rain ended, she went up to the chief while he was on his way between tents. "I know, I know," he said before she could speak. "It's those screams. If only there was more chloroform to make it easy for them. But headquarters seems to be ignoring this part of the war. I don't know whether it's because of the race of these men or just the usual lack of organization."

"Doctor, I'm asking for a chance to prove that I can really help."

He stopped in front of the next tent. "Well, I don't know whether, at your age, you could handle working next to me while I'm doing all this. I myself am having a problem with it. Excuse me, please."

As he started to go inside, she dashed in front of him. "No, I mean . . . it's so hard to say this and not sound crazy! But I know I can help you do something to prevent infections—"

"Look at my hand, please," he said suddenly.

"Your hand? Why? What has that—?"

"Just do it. How many fingers am I holding up?"

Hanna squinted at the wavering twin lines before they became one.

"Never mind answering. I can already see the effort you're making to focus. Look, you've had a blow to your head. You've been unconscious. Everything around you is very terrifying. And you are much too young to be in the middle of a war zone. I think you should—"

"Doctor, please listen to me! With the same water that we're using for our tea I can sterilize all these things you're using, the instruments, the bandages, the—"

"This is nonsense. I have to—"

"All I'm asking is that you give me an hour. Look, give me only a half hour to boil them in cooking pots before you use them again! Just—"

"I have no patience for this now! Go back to soothing these men while they wait their turn. That's woman's work, and even at your age you do it well. But I have been a

136

physician for twenty years. Please don't pretend to have special knowledge from who knows where."

"Tell me what you have to lose! Look how bad it is already. Won't you give me a chance to show you how to do something to stop these infections from spreading from one person to another?"

"Obviously you haven't had the slightest training in nursing whatsoever. Even the dullest mind knows that we must see large amounts of pus before there can be any healing. Now I don't care whose daughter you say you are! You will leave this area immediately and stay—"

While they were arguing, a new bombardment had begun. At that moment, a falling shell crashed into a nearby tent.

"Thank God it was empty!" exclaimed the field surgeon. But now there were new shells rocketing overhead. He glanced at a high stone outcropping that until now had been a protection for the station. "It's because of where they've moved those cannons! This is madness!"

While medics, and any of the wounded who could get up, searched for cover, the surgeon raced across the clearing. Cupping his hands, he shouted at an officer above. "You tell your men to roll their cannons away from my station! Look how it's drawing down the enemy's fire on us here."

"Can't be helped! The other way we were pouring fire into our own men fighting down by the woods. Move your White House!"

"Where? We've got no place to go. Don't you see how impossible that is? If any of my people are killed down here it will be *your* fault!"

"Is that so? Well, I don't know how all your hacking and sawing is good for them anyway. They tell me the men are dying from it quicker than they do from bullets."

"What's that? Are you blaming us?"

"No. But I'll tell you what. I won't run what passes for a hospital if you don't run what passes for a war."

Another explosion finished the quarrel by making the officer vanish. The surgeon did not wait an instant for the cloud of dust and stone bits to settle. As he clambered up the slope, Hanna seized one end of a stretcher while a medic took the other. Scrambling to the top of the ledge, they searched for the living among the dead.

"Over here!" cried the surgeon, who'd been wildly pulling corpses off a gasping man. Together they lifted him onto the stretcher and carried him down.

The surgeon went ahead of them to an operating tent. Hanna said nothing when, without stopping to wash, he got ready to pull a piece of metal from the gunner's stomach. But she could not bear to watch it being done this way.

As she went outside she saw another stretcher being brought into the encampment. Of course there had been wounded men brought in all day long. But this time the litter bearers weren't ordinary soldiers. They were officers. That told her who they might be carrying.

His hair had been wavy brown when last she'd seen him back in 1850. Now it was streaked with gray. Though his left arm looked shattered, that dear face showed no pain. Hanna ran alongside the litter, crying, "Papa. Oh, Papa!" She took his right hand but it was limp.

The officer in back was puzzled. "I thought he'd lost his daughter a long time ago. Isn't that right, Tim?"

"Yes, that's what I heard."

"No, he *didn't*. It's so hard to explain, but he didn't!" Her tears fell upon his face as she bent over him. "Oh, Papa, I'll take care of you."

She felt the hand tighten a little, saw the eyes flutter open. "So you did come, Dora," he murmured dreamily. "But how young you look. Like the day I first saw you at Fairweather Hall."

"Papa, no, it's me." Hanna's throat was so choked and pinched that her voice squeaked. "But Mama is coming too—I just know she is."

Amos Terwilliger lifted his head slightly. "Hanna? You're my baby come back to me?"

"Yes, Papa," she sobbed. "Yes!"

A thin little smile played upon his lips and he fell back unconscious.

Hanna raced ahead to the chief surgeon, her eyes flashing. "That's my father they're bringing in. I know you're going to amputate. I won't try to stop you. But I want you to let me sterilize everything first—the instruments, the stitching needles, the bandages, the thread! And, since you don't have sterilized gloves, promise me you'll wash yourself before you touch him!"

The exhausted chief surgeon threw up his hands. "All right. Just to humor you, I will. I cannot stop what I am doing now anyway, not even for an officer. Take a set of my instruments and go ahead."

"Thank you! Oh, thank you."

An aide helped her gather what she needed into a sheet. "Best let me go wit' you to the cooks," the man said. "They won't like you taking over their cooking fire and their pots jest when they fixin' to start gettin' up all the salt pork an' beans fo' supper. 'Sides which them iron kettles is heavy 'nuff to carry even without water."

Hanna soon found out just what a long haul it would be. All the cooking and drinking water for the camp was being taken from a single brook. But not more than twenty yards upstream men were using the bushes next to it for their toilet!

"You mustn't take the water from here or you'll make everybody sick as dogs!" she shouted at the cooks. They were scratching their heads when she left with the aide and two kettles to go farther upstream.

"I shouldn't have screamed at them," Hanna said, struggling with her kettle. "That's not the way to convince anyone, is it?"

"Yeah, but you did make 'em worry some. So maybe when you go back you could explain more quiet like so they listen to what you a-sayin'. I kin carry both. Let me get the other side of that."

"No, I can do it." But her lips trembled. "You actually seem to believe in what I'm doing. Why is that?"

"When I was a slave we couldn't have no real doctor, so we had us a kind of woods doctor. She used t' brew up the water with the medicine leaves and all the other good things in 'em jest like you're a-fixin' to do. She boiled them real long and hard too. And don't you know that sometimes it helped with the different miseries? How 'bout over here?"

"Yes, this is fine. There's someone very dear to me called the Conjure Woman," Hanna said as she tipped her kettle into the stream. "I guess you'd say she was a sort of woods doctor."

He broke into a big smile. "Now is that right? An' did you believe her?"

"You have to believe in someone who says you have powers, though I only wish I knew what they were. So, yes, I do. I'm just praying that she's around somewhere, watching and helping me."

"Sometimes I think that iffen one o' these sawbones doctors could just talk to a good woods doctor—"

"This one is full enough. But I can't pull it out by myself. Oh, we'll never be able to carry the two of these back to the fires!"

Just then a half dozen soldiers and cooks came hurrying along after them, calling out: "Here now, let us give you a hand with that."

"That's right. Why didn't anybody tell us this was for Colonel Terwilliger?"

"Now that's one white man we all will give up a lot more than a mealtime for!"

In no time kettles were sitting on roaring fires. Into one of them, Hanna threw the medical instruments. Into the other she tossed bandages, sponges, silk thread for stitches, and even two sheets she'd yanked off cots in a hospital tent.

Nervously she paced back and forth, trying to guess how

long they should be left to boil. When an inner voice told her she dared not wait any longer, Hanna had both kettles tipped over so that all the water poured out. As soon as everything had cooled, she grabbed the tongs and used them to lift out one of the sheets and spread it on dry ground. Then she spread the second sheet on top of the first and dropped the instruments on it, one by one. She gathered the sheets at the top. Now she was ready!

Hanna dashed back to the White House. Racing around madly, she found the chief surgeon coming out of his tent, tucking away a flask of brandy. "I've got them!" she said.

"Got what?"

What was wrong with the man? Was he drunk? "Everything for the operation!"

"That's over."

"What?"

"I mean that I took off the colonel's arm. Time will tell whether he pulls through or not." He looked away from her. "You will have to excuse me now. I have many other operations to perform tonight."

"But you *promised!*"

"You were hysterical. I had to say it to get you out of my hair." He waggled his finger at the linen bag. "Not that I expect to get any sleep, but if that is my bedsheet, I would like you to return it."

"Where is my Papa?"

The doctor pointed at a tent. "If he should awaken while you are with him, give him one of the blue mercury pills by the bedside. I'll look in on him in an hour or so."

"No, you will not," Hanna hissed at him violently. "I don't want you or anyone else going near my father!" She followed him across the clearing. "Do you hear what I'm saying? Answer me!"

"The whole army hears you. But of all people, it's the nurses and doctors who must stay the calmest. I must warn you that those who do not will soon fall prey to the diseases that are so easy to—"

She was not listening. Hanna ran into her father's tent and found him lying on his back, unconscious and shaking with chills. She ran out again, tore blankets off the doctor's own cot, ran back, and wrapped them around him, then climbed up on the narrow bed and held her father.

Any possibility of sleep ended when he began to babble. But his teeth clacked and the words were impossible to understand. At times he seemed to be leading his men on a charge into some dry gully . . . to be wrestling for a gun . . . to be trying to hold off an enemy soldier with his missing arm. When he fell back at last, sweat poured all over his twitching face.

Hanna wiped him with one of her sponges. She kissed his brow and began to sing the songs to him that he and Mama had so often sung together while she played the piano. She recited little poems that Aunt Ida had taught Mama and Mama had taught her. She told him about finding Johnny Appleseed again, and what a wonderful horse Papa had trained him to be. Twice she started to tell him about Rafe, but that was too painful, and right now she would not allow herself to think any more about it.

"Oh, Papa, you must be strong. Please promise me you're trying hard to come back to us."

"Is it really you, Hanna?" he asked in wonderment.

"Yes! Oh, yes, Papa, yes!"

"Where have you been all this time?"

"Oh, it's so hard to explain."

"Tell me, Hanna. I want to know."

Hanna talked. She talked for hours, but was he hearing any of it? "Papa, tell me if you know what I'm saying to you."

Bubbles appeared in the corners of his mouth. She put her ear to it. "Cinderella going to a ball," he whispered, just before his body began to shake again.

TEN

"Oh, my God! Hanna! Hanna!"

Rafe's voice jarred her awake. "You're safe!" she gasped, and threw herself into his arms. "The major told me you were killed, but I wouldn't believe him. I wouldn't."

"I thought *you* were dead!" he sobbed. "After that blast knocked me down, I got up and you were gone. I just couldn't stand it. I had to do something, so I ran off after the regiment. Hanna, it was awful. We were trying to sneak behind the enemy, but they were waiting for us. They pinned us in a crossfire and started mowing us down. We threw ourselves on them, firing and clubbing them and using our bayonets. I saw the colonel fall, but I couldn't get to him. Some of our men surrounded him and carried him out, but the rest of us stayed. We fought till there was nothing left to shoot with. You should have seen the way they looked at us, Hanna. They just couldn't believe black men could stand and fight like that. They left us to bury our dead, and we just got back. I came here to see how the colonel was."

Hanna looked at her father and bit her lip. "Oh, Rafe, he's so pale. He's lost so much blood! They don't have blood transfusions yet. They don't know anything about stopping wounds from getting infected. And what's more, they don't care! They even think it's *good!* What can I do for him? I just talk to him and hold him, but I have no idea whether Papa will get better or not."

"Perhaps I might tell you," declared the field surgeon, appearing at the tent. "Am I allowed to come in and look at your patient?"

When Hanna nodded, the surgeon bent over him. "The colonel's weak, naturally. But I believe he will pull through." He looked at her. "It seems you took it upon yourself to order the cooks to take their water farther up the stream from the makeshift latrines. You did well. I think that might be a good sanitary measure." He paused, then added, "And as for your notion of cleaning the instruments, well, it's time-consuming, but I don't think it would hurt. We do not, after all, know how so many fearsome diseases are spread." Then he shook his head at Rafe. "If I were you, private, I wouldn't hug your lady friend again where anyone might see. Nothing has changed *that* much, even on this side of the war."

"Sure, and how many centuries *will* it take to change?" Rafe said bitterly as the surgeon went out. He turned to her. "I've got to get back to my unit."

"No, don't," she cried. "Wait!" But he dashed away.

In the growing light of the new day, Hanna noticed how many wounded men were still lying about waiting for care. She glanced at her father, saw that he was peaceful, then went out among them.

The shelling had started again. Up on the ridge the men of a white regiment were crouching behind rocks firing at invisible foes. By midafternoon, however, Hanna could see them, for they came charging over the top screaming their wild rebel yells. Some of them fought their way into the medical encampment. Hanna, still wearing the captain's borrowed uniform, was shot at. As the bullet sailed past her, she tossed off her cap and shook out her hair.

"Gal, you shore live dangerous," declared a freckle-faced rebel, priming his musket as he ran past her. "Glad I didn't hit ye though. Too purty t' kill!"

Those were the last words to leave his lips before a bullet shot him down. Hanna ran to him, calling for a litter. The same aide who'd helped her before hurried over with it. As they lifted the rebel up, he smiled at her, saying, "Do ye cook some too?"

"Not too well, soldier, but tell me what you'd like." He made no reply, though he was still smiling at her. Hanna had to close his eyes forever.

She had little time after that to find out how the fighting was going. Both sides drove each other back and forth, leaving their wounded to lie where they had fallen until Hanna, along with the others, fetched them into the overcrowded medical station. There was so much to do and so little to do it with! The drugs to ease pain and the chloroform to make men unconscious during operations ran out. And this was only the beginning of an all-out, three-day fight! The soldiers stopped hurling themselves at one another at night, but those in-between hours did nothing to slow down the desperate work of doctors, nurses, and aides. These people grew so weary that they staggered about like drunks and tripped over new patients on the ground.

Through all of this, Hanna worked like a demon. She had

lost her sense of time and hardly knew whether it was day or night. She could not recall when she'd slept last or when she had eaten or with what she had moistened her dry, cracking lips.

It was while she was going from one patient to another that a terrible cramp gripped her stomach. As she doubled over, her head grew so light that she lost all awareness even before she crumpled to the ground.

"Of course I have no medical experience, but aren't you afraid this is cholera?" asked Major Clayton a few hours later. He was standing beside the chief surgeon just outside the special tent that had been put up for Hanna.

"Yes, I fear so."

"Then what's to be done?"

"Nothing, except to keep her apart from the others. We have no cure for this, just as we have no cure for so much else."

"Will she die?"

The chief surgeon sighed. "Some pull through on their own. Most do not. I think she thoroughly weakened herself before she fell ill." The chief surgeon paused. "She was a difficult woman to deal with. But a very brave one."

"At her tender age, she was hardly a woman yet."

"Oh, I disagree. War, I've discovered, has a way of making the young ones old. But at any rate, I thank you, Major, for the news that the supply wagons are finally arriving."

"Yes, a rider came in an hour ago to report. They've had a difficult time getting through and lost two wagons on the way to raiders. But I've sent out an escort to meet them. The person in charge of them, I believe, is the wife of the colonel. How is he faring?"

"He wakes for a few moments, then he sleeps. It's a good sign."

Hanna heard nothing of this conversation. Nor did she hear Mama hurrying toward her tent later, saying, "I don't understand. She told you she was our daughter? But our Hanna disappeared twelve years ago. My Lord! Could the Conjure Woman have been right? She always said that Hanna . . ."

Now Mama was anxiously standing over her.

"That poor wasted face. It's so hard to tell anything. But she does look something like my Hanna. Yet Hanna would be so much older. She would be twenty. No, it can't be her. And I know this is a terrible thing to say, but if the child is going to die, I don't *want* to believe she might be her! Please take me to my husband!"

"It gettin' near time to go, child," said the shadowy form that had entered Hanna's mind. "Y'all need to skip on ahead to the time where the doctors kin make you well again. Elsewise you goin' die real soon."

"But I've got to see Mama," said Hanna.

"Your mama done already seen you, sweetness."

"She . . . she has?"

"Oh, yes. She know it's you, only she ain't ready to say it to herself yet. By an' by, though, she will. She goin' talk to Rafe and find out who you is. And she goin' hear your Papa tell her how you must have come to him in a dream. An'

149

how that dream help make him so strong that he just would not give up the ghost to death. And Mama gonna say, 'That was my Hanna! She done come out of the future to bring my husband back to me! She's alive. My baby is alive somewheres jest like that old colored lady used to tell me she was—only I didn't believe her then.' She goin' write to Rosalie 'bout you. An' so will Rafe. An' they all goin' to be so happy for you that you done skip ahead again to where you kin be well."

"But how will they know?"

"Rafe's gonna tell them. Do you know where he be right now?"

"No."

"Why, he's roundin' up Johnny Appleseed for you. That ol' horse, he's goin' to be your skip ahead. You goin' get up on top of him and ride into the future. So let's get to it now."

"But I don't think I can move my body."

"Oh, yes, you kin. If I could get Rosalie Sims, with two bullets inside of her, to stand up and walk away from them slave trackers, then you kin do it too. You jest lean on the spirits and they'll help you all you needs."

"But I can't see any spirits."

"Neither did Mother Freedom that time, but they is here all around you. Now you just lean your soul on them and let your body rise."

"But I don't feel them!"

"That's jest what Rosalie said when she was being 'streperous. An' I told her what I'm tellin you. You just has to be willin' is all. Now why ain't you willin'?"

"Because I have to see Mama! I've got to see her!"

"Did I say you wouldn't? Did you think I was goin' to let you come all this way and not see your own mama? What do you take me for, child? Now you get into that body and be quick 'bout it. Believe me, you don't never want t' see anybody my age mad!"

"Yes'm," said Hanna in a tiny voice, and up her body rose.

"All right, now. Walk out o' this tent."

"Can't I walk regular?"

"You cain't see yourself yit, can you?"

"No."

"So how does you know you ain't walking reg'lar?"

"Cause I feel like Frankenstein!"

"What all is a Frankenstein? Never mind. Just keep a-goin'. That's right. That's good. Keep yo' hands out in front of you and mind the tent pole so you don't knock everything down. Kin you see anything yet?"

"No, but I think I hear Johnny Appleseed calling."

"Rafe's got him just a little ways farther on."

"He knows you're here?"

"'Course he knows. I come to him time to time just like I come to you! That boy so big in my heart. Ain't I already tol' you that?"

"Yes'm. Please don't be mad at me."

"Ain't mad. But I'm dead now. And it so much harder doin' things when you're dead than when you're alive. So move along now and try seein'. Kin you see?"

"I cain't."

"You talkin' like a little girl."

"I want my mama!"

"Your mama comin' presently. Move along now. You got people watchin' now, an' I don't want 'em decidin' to get in your way. Uh-oh, here come the sawbones. Get up on the horse now."

"Is he here?"

"Sho' he is. An' Rafe here's liftin' you into the saddle right now. Put the reins in the girl's hands, Rafe. Don't worry 'bout her fallin' off. The spirits gone stay wit' her awhile."

"Hanna! My Hanna! My baby!"

"That's Mama calling me! Why can't I see her!"

"Don't I wish I knew! But this here bein' dead got some of my powers all turned round. Use your own powers, child, afore Johnny Appleseed takes you skipping away."

"How?"

"Don't know. Cain't alway say how I does it neither. Just you let it come."

And Hanna did. She saw the tents and the many wounded still lying on the ground. She heard the cannons thundering again. She saw the surgeon looking on stupefied. And just in front of her now, she saw Mama!

Mama raised her hand and touched her leg. "My baby. My baby," she sobbed. Hanna leaned down so that Mama could reach her cheek. Hanna stretched out her hand to touch Mama's silken hair . . .

But Johnny Appleseed had been pawing the ground all the while. He gave a snort and took off so fast, Hanna nearly fell. Mama ran after her, stretching out with her fingertips.

But the horse no longer just galloped. He moved like the

wind. Hanna turned to look behind her, but the camp was disappearing, and her mother along with it. "Mama!" she called out just as she entered the darkness—a long, long darkness.

And then . . . why, then, bugles blared and drums rolled—and a marching band broke into "Rally Around the Flag!" Union soldiers by the hundreds marched before and behind her. There was cheering. Young women in bonnets waved. And stretched across a long picket fence was a painted banner that proclaimed:

ROCHESTER SENDS ITS BOYS
TO SAVE THE UNION!

Hanna felt terribly confused. What was she doing way up north in Rochester where her other family would live in the 1990s if this was still the Civil War? Had the Conjure Woman mixed everything up? Or was this a hallucination?

While her brain swam, her blurred eyes began to notice strange shapes behind the cheering lines of onlookers. She had to blink before those objects became clear enough to recognize as automobiles and buses! Now a truck rolled by with a swinging crane on it. At the end of that crane was a man wearing a baseball cap turned backward, seated in a chair behind a big camera! This march, she realized, was part of a movie!

"You on the horse!" the cameraman shouted. "What are you doing in this scene?"

153

Hanna opened her mouth to answer. But she could only gasp as the tremendous cramp began again. Her eyes rolled in her head, and swaying out of balance, she fell from the saddle.

ELEVEN

It was many days before Hanna looked up from a hospital bed and was able to give her name. But when no one could find a Terwilliger who'd ever heard of her, they came back. Clearing her head, she told them Anna Post—and that instantly brought Allan, Barbara, and Kevin to her bedside.

Her brother was jealous of having been left out of yet one more adventure. Her dad was pestered by some clerk who insisted on getting information right away about his insurance policy. Her mom couldn't decide whether to shower her with kisses or rebukes for leaving them without both.

Their excitement and the relief they felt at having her back alive and nearly well was tremendous. But Anna was terribly worried about Johnny Appleseed. What had happened to him? She couldn't rest until her dad told her that state troopers had taken the horse to their mounted police barracks. The stallion was being well cared for, but there'd be a charge for his hay and board.

"Another bill to pay," he sighed good-naturedly.

Kevin's eyes lit up. "I can't believe it—we have a horse!"

"It's *my* horse, Kevin."

He gave her a hard look. "You're not going to let me ride him?"

"How do you feel about my teaching you the right way to do anything?"

There was a long silence after that. While her brother was thinking it over, Allan Post put an arm over his shoulders, saying quietly, "Come on, Kevin. Let's go for sandwiches."

"But why now?"

"Because I said so."

As they went out, leaving Barbara Post alone with Anna, an awkward silence fell over the room. Mrs. Post had moved back to a place by the window, where she was clasping and unclasping her hands. "You're still my Anna," she said in a shaky voice. "I mean, you'll always be that. Do you know it?"

"Yes, Mom. Of course I do."

"Really?" Mrs. Post was crying now.

"Why are you doing that?"

"Why? Because I'm the one who needs reassurance now."

"Oh, Mom! I love you so much."

"You . . . you do?"

"Yes!" Anna put her arms out and her mother rushed into them.

"I want to hear the whole story. Don't you leave out a single thing! Help me to feel that I was there with you. Did you find everyone?"

"Yes, I found Rafe almost right away. You should see how wonderful he looks. I mean, looked."

"I'm so glad. And your Mama and Papa? Were you with them too?"

"Yes, I was. But Papa wasn't completely conscious. And then when Mama came, I wasn't. Oh, it was very strange. And it was hard too. But I *think* Mama knows I'm alive. I mean she finally learned that I—"

"Dearest, it's all right to say that she *knows*. You live in two different times. I realize that. And I'm . . . just so glad that you're back in *mine*. Are you happy at all to be here, my baby?"

Anna felt herself choking up. The last words Mama had called out to her were also "My baby."

"*Hanna! Hanna! My baby!*" Those sounds were echoing in her mind, coming down to her from a great distance in time. While Anna Post listened to her mom, Hanna Terwilliger listened to her mama. She knew in that moment that she was never going to stop feeling the love that would always be hers from both of them.

They were her mothers.

In your travels...

VISIT PLANET TROLL

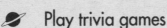